LIFE EXTINCT

A DCI SEAN BRACKEN NOVEL

JOHN CARSON

DI FRANK MILLER SERIES

Crash Point

Silent Marker

Rain Town

Watch Me Bleed

Broken Wheels

Sudden Death

Under the Knife

Trial and Error

Warning Sign

Cut Throat

Blood from a Stone

Time of Death

Frank Miller Crime Series – Books 1-3 – Box set

Frank Miller Crime Series - Books 4-6 - Box set

SCOTT MARSHALL SERIES

Old Habits

LIFE EXTINCT

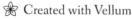 Created with Vellum

For the real Jim Brown

ONE

They might have had one for the road if it wasn't for the weirdo sitting watching them.

'He might be waiting for a girl,' Dr Angela Monroe said, sipping the last of her lager.

'Yeah, right.' Myra Taylor sipped out of her own pint glass, looking over the rim at the man, who was now averting his gaze.

'See? That's what we get for being two beautiful young women out drinking on their own.'

'Young? Twenty years ago maybe.'

Angela laughed. 'I've already turned forty, and you're not even there yet. We don't exactly have to go looking for a retirement home just yet.'

William Potter, their boss and sometime drinking

partner, came across with three glasses and sat down. 'Cheers,' he said, raising his glass of whisky.

'Cheers,' the women said, clinking glasses.

'Do you want to go and live in America?' Myra saw the man looking at them out of the corner of her eye.

'Me? No. I'm quite happy here. I don't want to go anywhere else. I have everything I need, Angela said.'

'Except a man.'

'You and me both. But there's time for the dating scene later.'

'Speed dating maybe?' Myra asked.

'Sounds about right. I set the bar too high a long time ago. Now I want to set it a wee bit lower. Just to have some fun.'

'Hairy Houdini from Corstorphine was a bit of a laugh, but we only had the one date after the speed-dating thing. He's a magician and a mind reader. He wanted to show me a trick when we were having dinner. He told me he could take a cotton hankie out of my handbag without me seeing, but when he reached into a pocket, he pulled out a skimpy pair of knickers He said, "Oops, wait a minute," and then he pulled a cotton hankie out of another pocket.'

'Did you feel a breeze afterwards?' Angela asked.

'Nope. We had a laugh, and I took his number and promised to call him.'

'And you haven't called him, I assume?' Potter said, smiling.

'Let's just say, if he's a mind reader, he would already have known I wasn't going to call.'

'Why does he call himself *Hairy Houdini*?'

'He has a beard. The real Houdini didn't have a beard, and he said it's so people will be able to look back years from now and distinguish the difference between them. I think they'll be able to do that anyway because Hairy's a load of shite.'

Angela laughed. 'Well, I went out with a magician one time, and he said he would make my virginity disappear. I told him, "Little bit late for that, pal."'

They laughed, then Myra looked directly at the staring man, feeling anger rising up inside her.

'He keeps looking over. I'm going to ask him what his problem is.' She got up before Angela could stop her and walked over to the table. The man, who looked to be in his forties, with a short beard and black hair, looked away, towards the TV that sat on a shelf in a corner.

'Why don't you take a photo? It'll last longer,' Myra said.

The man turned slowly, took hold of his pint and casually sipped it before looking her in the eye.

'Don't flatter yourself,' he said to her.

'Cheeky bastard. Keep your eyes on that fucking TV and not on me and my friend.'

'Or what?'

Myra leaned in closer and looked him straight in the eye. 'You don't want to find out.'

She straightened up and walked away and sat back down. The man finished his pint and picked up a jacket from the bench seat he was sitting on and he walked out, not looking at the two women.

'You chasing my customers out, Myra?' said the barman, a big, round Irishman, with a grin.

'This is our local, Paddy, and we want to feel comfortable.'

'Too right. If he comes in here again, I'll boot his feckin' arse out the door.'

The two women chatted some more, then Angela looked at her watch. 'I'm up early. I want to go home now.'

'Fine by me. What about you, William?'

'I'm off too. Up early in the morning.'

'Couple of lightweights,' Myra said, chuckling.

They said goodnight to Potter outside and

walked down Canongate, in the opposite direction to Potter.

'I love the light nights,' Myra said. 'The summer solstice is tomorrow. I wish it could be like this year-round.'

'Beats walking through snow, that's for sure.'

They turned into Coopers Close, went through the short tunnel underneath the building above and came out into a small close. It was still light, despite the late hour, but the buildings surrounding them created shadows.

Angela heard the running footsteps first, and she turned round and let out a noise that was half-shout, half-scream.

It was Beardy, running at them. The man from the pub now had his jacket on, keeping his hands free.

'You bitch,' he said to them, and Myra assumed he was addressing her, but he was drawing his arm back as he got closer to Angela.

Myra stepped in front of her friend and blocked the punch. She wrapped her arm around the man's right arm and stepped in close and headbutted him, but he ducked and her head connected with the top of his.

'Run!' she shouted to Angela, who didn't need to be told twice.

Beardy's left hand struck out blindly and he grabbed her hair. Myra twisted round and brought her right elbow up into the man's face. She heard his nose break and his grip loosened as he let out a yell.

She turned quickly and kicked him hard between the legs as he held his face. Now he went down onto his knees and she kicked him in the guts.

He toppled over. Myra took her phone out and put it close to Beardy's bleeding face.

'I'm going to study this photo when I get home. If I ever see your face again, I'll fucking rearrange it. Do you understand me?'

Nothing.

She stepped back and kicked the man hard. 'I said, do you understand? If you don't answer me, I'm going to stomp on your kneecap.'

'Yes,' the man said, his voice barely a grunt.

'Good. I'm going to walk down there, and you're going to go in the opposite direction. If you attempt to come after me, I will kick you so hard in your privates, you'll never be able to achieve an erection again. Got it?'

Wisely, he nodded.

'Do yourself a favour: never come back into our

pub again. If you do, I'll kick your arse in front of them and make you squeal like a little girl.'

She stood up straight, put her phone away and walked down the hill, following in her friend's footsteps. Myra was confident that the man wasn't following her.

Two men were standing outside the aparthotel at the bottom of the close, looking at her. Angela was nowhere to be seen. Which wasn't surprising, Myra thought, smiling to herself.

When she was walking down Holyrood Road, with no fear of her attacker catching up, Myra took her phone out and sent a text to Angela: *You okay?*

A few seconds later, she got a text back. *In the flat. Thank you! Love you, sister.*

Myra smiled again. *C U l8r.*

They both lived in the same apartment block near the parliament, so she relaxed when she got into the building and took the lift up to her own floor.

She went into the bathroom and looked in the mirror. She was pleased to see the only thing wrong with her was some hair out of place.

'Did he really think he was going to get the better of me?' she said to her own reflection. 'Not a chance.'

Myra felt exhilarated. She went to bed and stared at the ceiling for a little while.

TWO

'I told you, Sean, we're fine,' Catherine Bracken said to her ex-husband.

Bracken was looking out of the living room window, down to the Water of Leith. At the Constitution Street bridge and the floating restaurant beyond. He liked the summer nights, when the sun didn't set until late.

'I know you are, but I just wanted to check on you. You know I'm only a phone call away if you need help.'

Sarah, his daughter, had moved back in with her mother the previous winter after an incident that shook them all.

'You told me that the last time. And the last. And the last.'

He turned from the window and smiled at her. 'That bad?'

'Yes.' She smiled back at him.

'Is everything okay between you and...?' He nodded to the door to the living room through which Catherine's boyfriend had disappeared a few minutes ago.

'Who? Santa Claus? No, it can't be him; he would come down the chimney if we had one.'

He shook his head. 'I meant...'

'Leon. You can feel comfortable calling him by his first name.'

Ed Bracken sat in a chair in the living room near the TV, which was off. 'Aye, or you can take him into one of your interview rooms and "interview" him,' he said, using finger quotes.

'One thing's for sure: I'll be giving you an interview later,' Bracken said to his father.

'You're threatening me in front of witnesses? Dear oh dear, you're slipping a wee bit there, son. Besides, my boy here would be all over you like a rash.'

Max, Ed's German shepherd, raised his head for a second, but sensing there was no immediate threat, put his head back down.

'You're lucky you've got that big dog.'

Catherine smiled. 'Nothing changes with you two, does it?'

'I've got to keep him on his toes, love,' Ed said.

'Right, I'm off,' Sarah Bracken said, coming into the living room and putting on a lightweight jacket.

'Where are you going?' Bracken asked his daughter. She was going on twenty-two, but he still thought of her as five.

'Don't worry, Dad, I'll be fine.'

'Aye, the lassie will be fine,' Ed chipped in, earning a thrown dagger from Bracken's eyes.

'A man has a right to worry about his lassie,' Bracken countered.

'I never worried about you. And you're a big lassie,' Ed said.

'You're so funny.'

'Listen to you two,' Catherine said. 'What is Leon going to think?'

Bracken and Ed looked at each other, silently suggesting that neither of them gave a monkey's what Leon thought.

Then the man of the hour came back into the living room, larger than life at five foot six.

'Hope I didn't miss anything,' he said, beaming a smile at Bracken.

'My son was just talking about how he's going to

take you somewhere quiet with a piece of hosepipe and give you a lecture on the perils of upsetting my granddaughter.'

Max was up now, standing in front of his master, not quite baring his teeth but ready to spring into action at a second's notice.

Leon laughed and pointed at Ed. 'Always being the wit, Ed, I see.'

Bracken stood behind Leon and drew a finger across his own throat, imitating what was about to happen to the old man when they were left together.

'Certainly half,' Bracken answered. 'Don't pay attention to him, Leon.' *Just because I'm eight inches taller and probably three stone heavier than you, doesn't mean to say I'm going to kick your head in if you mess my ex-wife or my daughter about.*

'Well, it was nice meeting you all, but I really should be going. Thank you for dinner, Catherine.'

'You don't have to thank me, Leon. Drink tomorrow night?'

'I'll give you a call. We have rehearsals tomorrow night. Maybe later in the week?'

'Absolutely. Let me see you out.' Catherine ushered her boyfriend out of the living room, closing the door behind her. They heard the front door opening and the voices got muted.

'That'll be Mum apologising for you two,' Sarah said. Then she walked to the dog and Max wagged his tail furiously. 'No, not you, lovely boy.'

'Oh, come on, we were just pulling his leg,' Bracken said. 'Him more than me.' He nodded to his father.

Sarah looked at him. 'Dad, just by being in the same room as Leon, you make him feel intimidated.'

'Nothing I can do about that, except not be in the same room as him. But your mother invited me and Methuselah over to meet her new beau.'

'Beau? Dad, you know I love you, but please don't ever use that word in front of my friends.' Sarah looked at her father for confirmation.

'I know, I know, students these days don't use big words. It's all shortcuts in a text. We're breeding a nation of non-spellers.'

'Correct me if I'm wrong, but I don't think "spellers" is a word.'

Ed laughed. 'She got you there, son.'

'Well, don't let me keep you, honey. Tell your friends I said hi.'

'Yeah, I'll pass that on.' She smiled and gave her father and grandfather a peck on the cheek, and rubbed Max's head. 'Tell Chaz I said hi and I'm sorry she couldn't make it tonight.'

'I will. We can have a drink sometime.'

'I look forward to it.'

And then she was out of the living room, and Bracken felt a sudden pang of sadness, thinking back to when his daughter was a little girl. He had some wonderful memories, but it all seemed like such a long time ago. It reminded him of his own mortality, and how one day she would have to say goodbye to him as he departed this life for another.

Then he snapped himself out of it as Catherine came back into the room.

'Leon said he had a good time,' she said. 'You boys wanting one for the road?'

'Magic,' Bracken said. 'I'm glad the wee man had a good time.'

'You're not going to start on about his height, are you?' Catherine said.

'Me? It's just a term of endearment. Like I call *him* wee man.' He nodded towards Ed.

'You don't call me that, cheeky bugger. And you'd better not start now.'

'A'right, wee man, keep your skids on.'

'Maybe he's had enough, Catherine, love,' Ed said.

'A tinnie and a wee chaser, Cath, if you don't mind,' Bracken said, ignoring Ed.

'Aye, go on then,' Ed agreed, apparently having had his arm twisted. 'I'm getting a taste for that fine malt that Leon brought along. He did say we could help ourselves to it.'

'I thought he told you to keep your filthy mitts off it?' Bracken said to the old man.

'It's all in the interpretation.'

They both agreed that Leon had inferred they could get wired into the expensive Scotch. Bracken saw Leon leaving his whisky as the precursor to leaving a toothbrush and a change of underwear and he felt a jolt inside. *Christ, how can I feel jealous?* he thought.

Catherine left, going through to the kitchen, which was off the living room.

'I think Chaz would have liked Leon,' Ed said as Max lay down again.

'Yeah. Being on the night shift is a pain.'

'Is she still thinking about changing jobs?'

'She is,' Bracken said, sitting down. 'She's on the fence, though. I mean, she has the degree to do it, but it's a big change, going to work in a lab during office hours.'

'At least she wouldn't be working on a Sunday night, like tonight.'

'That's a big deal. She's going to make the decision soon. She just needs a little push.'

'Then give her a gentle nudge, son.'

Catherine came back with two glasses.

'Cheers,' Ed said.

'Up yours,' Bracken said and they both drank.

THREE

When Chaz Cullen pulled up to the house in the mortuary van, everything was done and dusted. A police uniform had smashed the window in the front door to gain entry, he had found the deceased on the living room floor, the police doctor had been called and declared the victim life extinct, and now Chaz was the icing on the cake.

'This must be a record for you, Chaz,' the uniform said to her. 'It's only ten-thirty and you've been called out on a shout. Night shift starts at ten, doesn't it?'

'It does. It beats sitting about doing nothing. Or even worse, knitting. I'd rather be busy.'

'Your wish is my command. Potential crime scene,' the uniform told her. 'It may be a case for your boyfriend, if the pathologist deems it something not quite natural.'

'We get sudden deaths all the time, Ian. Not all of them are murder.'

'Walk in the park for Bracken, though, isn't it?' he said, smiling.

'Yes. And will you please stop referring to him as my "boyfriend"?'

'What is he then?'

Chaz shrugged. There was no other answer than 'boyfriend', but considering he was forty-five and she was thirty-two, it didn't seem right. Maybe if they were teenagers, but it just sounded like she was dating a schoolboy. One day, if things worked out between them, she could call him her husband, but that was a way off yet.

'Let's just get inside and see to our cadaver, shall we?' she said. She took the gurney out of the back of the van, the wheeled legs dropping down automatically. There was a black body bag on top. Chaz always thought about her own mortality when she was called out to any scene. Sometimes she dwelled on it too much, instead of thinking of the positive side of life.

The uniform led her into the terraced house. She thought that East Craigs was a nice neighbourhood, tucked away between Corstorphine and Barnton.

The house was in the middle of a row of four terraced houses built in the 1980s. The short hallway led into the living room, where the young man was still lying on the carpet in front of a gas fire that wasn't on.

'The doc said there doesn't seem to be anything obvious that would make it more than a sudden death, but the pathologist, Dr Green, will determine that when she gets this lad on the steel table.'

'How old is he?' Chaz asked, feeling sorry for the young man who had left earth behind way too early.

'Driving licence says he's twenty-eight. Colin Paisley.'

'Does he live alone?'

Ian shook his head. 'Neighbour says he has a live-in girlfriend who works late sometimes. We're waiting for her to arrive home, but I would rather him not be lying on the floor if that's possible.'

'Flex those big guns of yours then, Ian, and help me get him into the bag.'

They worked the corpse with care, respecting the young man even in death, and Ian helped her manoeuvre the gurney back out to the van. Neighbours were looking, some women standing with a hand over their mouth.

Chaz got in behind the wheel and started the engine, switching on the headlights, and drove slowly out of the small, dead-end street. It was certainly a dead-end for the young man in the back of the van.

She drove along Maybury Drive in the anony-mous van, unaware of a red Audi TT heading in the opposite direction, driven by a young woman whose life was about to be changed forever, and she wouldn't be aware of it for the next few minutes. Then it would hit her between the eyes.

'How's it going back there, Colin?' Chaz asked. She liked to speak to them, but only when she was driving alone. If young Jim was with her, then they would listen to the radio or crack some jokes.

Tonight it was a Sunday and she was the one on-call, so she was the sole transporter of death. That was a term Bracken had used, making her sound like some hit-woman who roamed the streets of Edin-burgh taking out bad guys.

'Did you enjoy your life? It's hellish having it cut short, and I'm sorry your girlfriend is going to be given the bad news by Ian, but at least he's compas-sionate. When he's not being a dick. But she's in good hands. It's going to feel like her whole world has crashed down, because it has, but she'll pick herself up eventually.'

She turned onto Maybury Road, heading down towards South Gyle. Cutting along the Broadway, she connected with Broomhouse.

'I have a boyfriend, thanks for asking. What's that? Do I love him? Of course I do. But that's like asking "Do you have the cooker on?" when you're about to start baking a cake. It starts off at a low peep and gets hotter the longer it goes on. We're taking things steady right now. Sean still lives in a guest house. He made an offer on a couple of flats but got pipped at the post. I'm thinking about asking him if he wants to move in with me, but not right now. It's been six months, and you know what it's like when things are going smoothly: you do something to jinx it. So I'm happy with the way things are going for now.'

She listened to the radio for a bit as she connected with the Western Approach Road.

'I hope you were happy with your girlfriend, Colin,' she said as she neared Lothian Road. 'You obviously were happy enough to move in with her, but were you happy now? I hope you were. I hope you didn't have a fight before she went to work today. You never know when it's going to be your last day, do you? You leave for work, don't tell your partner you love them and then it's all over. I didn't tell Sean I loved him before I went to work today. I meant to shoot him off a text telling him, but he was going to Catherine's flat to meet her new boyfriend. I was invited along, of course, because Catherine and I get along fine. I've met her a few times now, and Sarah was there, so she would have been sort of a buffer, and we get along well. But I didn't want Sean to think I was feeling jealous and had to send him a text just because he was in the company of his ex. His dad, Ed, was going too, and Max. I love them both. Ed is a wonderful man and he'll be a great father-in-law. But listen to me, wittering on about my private – oh, shite!'

Chaz jammed the brakes on as a car cut her off on the approach to Lothian Road. She leant on the horn and the car crawled towards the traffic lights. It was a black BMW with blacked-out windows. The lights turned to green and the front two cars turned into Lothian Road, but the BMW drove slowly, antagonising her. What if it was drug dealers inside? Hitting the horn was a reflex. If the bastard got out, she would tell him who she was and that if he wasn't more fucking careful, she'd be driving *him* to the mortuary.

The car shot off and Chaz held back, just long enough for the lights to change back to red. She looked in her mirror but didn't see any headlights behind her. It wouldn't do to piss off more than one driver tonight.

Her heart was beating faster now. 'Bloody drivers, eh, Colin? You won't have to worry about that now, though. But you probably wish that you could still have that as a problem. It's hard. We take everything in life for granted, and then one day, it's all over. People say, live each day as if it's your last, and I wonder if you lived today like it was your last. Probably not. If it was me, I would be well arsed by now. Bottle of Bacardi, nice Chinese takeout, get Sean to make slow love to me. No, make that fast love. Faster than usual, anyway. I try to tell him it's a marathon, not a sprint, but sometimes he gets so eager. For a man of forty-five, he's quite athletic, but it's a bit like going to the shows and getting on the waltzers when you've had six pints and a Ruby Murray. Once a night is enough. But that's what I would do. Go out with a bang, as it were.'

She stared at the red light, wondering where Sean was at that moment. Was he still down with Catherine? Or had he gone for a swift pint down the Shore with Ed and the dog? Did pubs still let dogs in down in Leith, now it was slowly being gentrified? She knew Sean still liked going into a man's pub. He and Ed frequently went along to the Diggers at Ardmillan, the nickname for the pub, which came from the gravediggers who used to pop in for a pint when they were working in the cemetery opposite. That's what Ed had told her, but maybe that was just a myth. Whatever it was, she had persuaded Sean to take her there one night and they had got blootered together.

A horn sounded behind her, and she sat up straight, startled for a second. She thought it was the BMW, but he couldn't have got back on the road and made it all the way back along here in one cycle of the lights. Could he?

She put the van in gear and floored it through the lights, watching as the headlights behind her got smaller. Whoever it was didn't want to pick a fight. It was merely a gentle *The lights are green for go, mate* type of honk. Not like hers.

They weren't that far from the Cowgate now, as she turned into Bread Street.

'Do you think I should broach the subject again, Colin?' There was a metal panel behind her separating her from the freight section, but she still liked to think the corpses were closer to her. 'Asking Sean to move in with me?'

Two men were pushing each other around on the pavement outside the Western Bar at the West Port, maybe fighting over who was going to take a stripper home. They stepped out into the road and she was about to lean on the horn again, but slowed down instead and zipped past as they made their way back onto the pavement.

She drove through the Cowgate, where she eventually pulled into the small car park of the city mortuary.

'Here we are Col–' she started to say but cut herself short.

There was a light on upstairs.

The headlights lit up the roller door over on the left of the brick and concrete building, and she sat and stared at the light on in one room. Somebody must have left it on, and because she had left when it was still light outside, she hadn't noticed it. Plus, she had reversed the van out, so she was concentrating.

With her heart pounding a lot more than Colin's was, she inched the van forward, keeping one eye on the upstairs window whilst trying not to knock the roller door out of its frame.

She hit the clicker attached to the sun visor and

the door started its ascent. She had left the lights on downstairs in the receiving bay and near the offices. She was daft, but not that daft.

Should she call Sean, just to let him know what she had seen?

'What do you think, Colin? Call my boyfriend and act like a scared wee lassie? Or go upstairs and switch the light off? What's that you say? Did I leave the light on? No, of course it wasn't me. Don't be silly. Pamela must have popped round and forgotten to put it off. Or maybe it was you who did it. Your spirit flew along here just to make sure the place wasn't in darkness for me.' She shook her head. 'Silly cow.'

The van made it inside and she hit the clicker for the door to come back down and switched the van's engine off and killed the headlights. The receiving bay was in total silence, like she had just brought a spaceship into the mothership and she was the only one in space. In space, nobody will hear you –

There was a knock on the driver's side window. She jumped, the scream that would have parted somebody's hair caught in her throat. Later on, she would count herself lucky she hadn't shat herself, but in that moment, she would swear her hair had turned white.

She turned to look at the figure standing there, expecting it to be one of the dead who had climbed out of the fridge.

'Chaz, it's me, Jim.'

Chaz held her breath for a few seconds longer before feeling it rush out in one huge whoosh. She flung the door open. Jim fucking Brown. The newest and youngest member of the team. Chaz obviously needed to teach him a few things about being a mortuary attendant.

'Fucking hell, Jim,' Chaz said.

He smiled at her. 'Good evening to you too,' he said, grinning.

'Daft bastard,' Chaz said, charging on with her verbal assault. Her fright was being masked by anger. 'What in the name of Christ are you doing here?'

'I was upstairs looking for something in my locker.'

Chaz felt relief sweep through her, realising it wasn't a zombie walking about upstairs. Well, it was *this* zombie, but she would rather it be him than a real one.

'You alright? You look like you've seen a ghost,' he said, his grin even wider.

'I took Krav Maga you know. Wee bastard.' She slammed the van's door shut.

'Aw, come on. I didn't mean to scare you. I was just picking up something I left on Friday. It's an old CD.'

'You mean to say you came back here late on a Sunday night to get some manky old CD? How daft do you think I am?' She realised her words sounded accusatory. Like she was insinuating he had been fiddling with one of the corpses.

'My girlfriend's out in the car. We're going back to her place because her mum and dad are away for a week. This CD is brilliant. It's my dad's. He made it years ago. It's all eighties tunes.'

'Never heard of Spotify?'

'My girlfriend has a little boombox thing from when she was a wee girl and it still works. These songs are all classics: Simply Red "Holding Back the Years", bit of Kenny G in there. Whitesnake "Is This Love". If this doesn't put her in the mood, she's dead inside.'

Chaz smiled despite herself. The first time Sean had made love to her, they had been playing music and Stevie Nicks had been on, singing "Sleeping Angel" from the *Fast Times at Ridgemont High* soundtrack. Which was an eighties tune.

'Don't keep the lady waiting, Jim,' she said, going round to the back of the van.

'You want a hand while I'm here?'

'No thanks. Colin and I can manage from here. Go and have a good time.'

'Colin?'

She nodded sideways to the van. 'My passenger. I'll fridge him, then I'm off to make a cuppa. Keep my fingers crossed there's not another call-out tonight.'

'Right. I'm sorry about scaring you, Chaz. I honestly thought you had seen me.'

'It's all right. Luckily, I've got nerves of steel.'

'Aye, well...' He grinned.

Chaz put a finger close to her lips. 'Just go, Jimmy.' She watched him go to the staff entrance door. '''Til Tuesday,' she said.

'You not in tomorrow?'

'Look them up, Jim. If you like eighties music.'

He winked at her and let himself out.

She felt a sense of relief as she wheeled out the guest who had joined the others for the summer solstice gathering and took him through to the fridges.

After dealing with Colin, she went into the office to make a coffee, then realised that she'd left her sandwich box in her car.

The mortuary was built up higher than street

level, so the small car park had a hedge running around it for privacy. That's why Chaz parked on the street, so if anybody assaulted her, maybe people would see it happening and intervene. Or at the very least film it for YouTube.

She walked round to the car and saw a flyer on the windscreen. But when she took it off, she saw it wasn't a flyer but a note.

Addressed to her.

A piece of white paper, folded in half, with her name written in black in capital letters.

She lifted it, got in her car and locked the door. She opened it and started reading.

You could have saved me, Chaz. If you had spoken up sooner. You could have saved me. I wouldn't be in a box in the ground if you had said something sooner. I don't know how you sleep at night. We need to talk.

Chaz realised she had been holding her breath and she let it out in a rush.

She hurried back inside, knowing she was definitely going to call Sean.

Tell him about the dead man who wanted to have a talk with her.

FOUR

'Thanks for coming round,' Chaz said to Bracken. 'Terry Jones comes in early and he told me to just get off, and he would take the van out if they got a call.' They both yawned. Both tired, he because he hadn't been up long and she because she had finished her night shift. It had just gone six-thirty.

'You don't have to thank me,' he said, sitting down on her couch and accepting the coffee. She had a beer, the elixir that would help her sleep.

'I know it's early and you were meeting Catherine last night and you were probably up late —'

He held up a hand. 'She only wanted me and Ed to meet Leon because he'll be around Sarah. I told her, Sarah isn't six anymore. But she wanted us all to meet him, so it wouldn't be awkward if we bumped into each other in the street. That's all it was. And Ed and Max and I weren't in late, trust me.' *We did arse what was left of a good bottle of whisky,* he thought, but edited that part out.

'I love you, Sean, just in case you weren't feeling it.'

He looked at her. 'I love you too, but I can tell from your body language and demeanour that something's troubling you.'

'You never step out of your detective shoes, do you?'

'It's kept me alive so far.'

'It's this.' She put her beer bottle down, took the note out of her pocket and passed it across to him. He read it and looked at her.

'Where did you get this?'

'I found it last night. On my windscreen.'

Bracken read it again. 'Who is it from? What does it mean, "You could have spoken up sooner"? Who's in a box –'

Now it was Chaz's turn to interrupt him. 'One question at a time.' She picked up her beer bottle and took a drink before she started answering. 'If it was written by the dead man, his name is Howard Wilson. He was a young man who had collapsed in the street and he was pronounced dead at the hospital. Heart attack, they said. So they brought him to us. Standard procedure for a sudden death. Then, when he was on the gurney under a sheet, I thought he moved. I mean, that's not unusual in itself, but I thought I heard a groan. Pamela and I examined him and there was no sign of life. But his temperature indicated that he might have been alive at the hospital and some doctor who was rushed called the TOD. There was a big lawsuit – it was in the papers and the family were upset – but there was just the barest possibility that he was still alive when he was brought to us. The family settled out of court, and that was the end of it.'

'Except Howard Wilson now thinks that you should have to pay for your negligence.' He put the piece of paper on the coffee table. 'Could it be one of your colleagues playing a prank?'

'No. The mortuary is shut on a Sunday, except in extreme instances, and I was the only one working. Except...' She hesitated for a moment.

'What?'

'The new guy was there. Jim Brown. He's been with us for a few months, and I saw one of the lights on upstairs when I came back with the van and he was inside. Getting a CD from his locker, he said.

There were no cars in the car park, but he said his girlfriend was outside in his car so he must have been parked close to me. Maybe he did it as a prank.'

'When did this happen, the Wilson case?'

'Five years ago, give or take.'

'How old is this Brown kid?'

'Twenty-four, I think.'

'He would have been nineteen when this happened. Maybe he read about it in the papers and he's decided to write this note to you to wind you up. You lot didn't mess with him when he started working there, did you?'

She looked sheepish for a moment. 'Well, we did have one of the other attendants, Monica, lie under a sheet, and when Jim pulled the tray out, she sat up. He nearly pissed himself.'

'There you are then. I think he's getting you back.'

'It's a bit extreme,' she replied, knowing that answer made sense.

'It's better than him putting a laxative in your coffee.'

'Good point. You want to listen to some eighties music?'

FIVE

Bob Long co-owned the guest house with his wife, Mary, but being a detective would always be in his blood, despite the fact he had been medically retired.

Having his old friend Sean Bracken living here temporarily had stopped him from going over the edge. He liked chewing the fat with him. Like now, when he brought two mugs of coffee out into the back garden.

It was light, but this north-facing garden was still in shade. Still, it was warm.

'Who stole your ball?' Bob said, putting the two mugs on the small table. He sat down beside his friend. Max was lying on the patio at Bracken's feet, panting heavily after chasing the ball back and forth for five minutes. 'You look like you should be listening to "Careless Whisper".'

'I went round to Chaz's. She got off early and she told me a dead man had left a note on her car at the mortuary.'

Bob took a sip of the coffee and waited for the punchline. None came.

'I hate to ask, but what dead man?'

'Howard Wilson.' Bracken took his own coffee. Looked at his watch. Seven-eighteen.

'Isn't that the bloke who was dead, but they thought he wasn't dead, then he was dead again?'

'Say that three times fast. But yes, that's the same guy.'

'But he was really dead, wasn't he?'

'Yes.'

'But he wrote Chaz a note?' Bob said.

'Fucking hell, Bob, I don't know how the force is managing to stumble along without you.'

'Cheeky bastard. You're the one talking in riddles. Dead man not dead, but then dead again, and now he's no' deid. Make up your bloody mind.'

'Look, it's simple. Like you. He was dead, but they thought they saw signs of life, but he was still dead. Now somebody's written a note and left it on Chaz's windscreen at the mortuary.'

'Simple? Listen, son, I was solving complex murders when you were still spit-polishing your boots at Tulliallan.'

'Don't talk pish. You're only five years older than me.'

'Still. Bloody insults, eh?'

'Sorry, pal.' Bracken lifted his coffee mug and clinked it against Bob's.

'Don't worry about it. I'd write your name on the lavvy wall if it wasn't me who would have to clean it off again. So what's really eating you?'

Bracken sipped the brown liquid, feeling it start to make him feel more human. 'Ed and I were round at Catherine's last night.'

'Aye, you said you were going. What happened? You get pished and blurt something out to her?'

'What? No, nothing like that. We got arsed into her new boyfriend's whisky after he left. The good stuff. Ed's lying in his pit with a head he can't lift off the pillow. Hence Maxy boy here is out with me.'

'Ah, that explains things,' Bob said, bending over to pet the dog. Max wagged his tail.

'What things?' Bracken said, lifting the mug as he felt his cheeks burn.

'Oh, come on, son, you can't fool me: you're jealous of Catherine moving on, despite the fact you've been divorced for six years and moved away to work in Fife. She was dating before, wasn't she?'

'Yeah, well, I didn't expect her to be like a nun. Maybe it's because of what happened with those blokes six months ago. I feel overprotective.'

'Is everything okay between you and Chaz?'

Bracken hesitated before answering. 'Aye, of course it is. She's just worried about the note, and her head is full of this job. She'd be working in the hospital in a lab. Less stress, less hassle and no night shift. It's more money too.'

'What is she waiting for?' Bob sat back in his chair.

'I'm not sure, to be honest. She just said she's still thinking about it, but I told her, the position won't be open forever.'

'You know what women are like: it takes them two hours to get ready to go out on a Saturday night,' Bob said, then they heard a noise from the back door and Max looked up.

'Not all women,' Kara Page said.

'I was just quoting a line from a movie, wasn't I, Sean?'

'No, you were being a sexist bastard,' Bracken said.

'I obviously meant Mary, not you, Kara.' Bob

quickly looked round to see if Mary was standing behind the DSup, but his wife was nowhere to be seen. She was still inside dishing up breakfast.

'Oh, Bob, you just dig yourself a deeper hole,' Kara said, smiling at him.

'He made me say it,' was Bob's last line of defence before pleading insanity.

'I would have you cracked like a nut in an interview room in five minutes,' Kara replied.

'No doubt. You want a coffee?'

'Is this your way of grovelling after insulting all women on the planet?' Kara said.

'It is indeed.'

'You know how I like it. A little extra milk this morning, please.'

Bob got up from his seat, offering it to his guest, and went back inside to get the coffee. Kara rubbed Max's head before the dog lay down again.

'How's the house coming along?' Bracken said, sure he had asked the night before, but the whisky had dulled his brain a little bit.

'You asked me that last night when you and Ed came in four sheets to the wind.'

'I only drink to keep the old man company. And it was hardly four sheets.'

'The term "tipsy" is reserved for old ladies who've been at the sherry bottle.'

'What was your answer?'

'To which question? Would I like a dance or how is my house coming along?'

Bracken felt his cheeks go on fire again. Big, bad Bracken, hard man, until a woman embarrassed him. 'Dance? You're not being serious.'

Kara laughed. 'I am. And I think you might have actually gone for it had you not been holding Ed up. Where is he, by the way?'

'Still in bed. He can't handle his drink like he used to.'

'That makes two of you. But to put you out of your misery, they're putting in the plasterboard this week. It will be another few weeks. Who knew it would take so long to get the repairs off the ground? Bloody red tape.'

'Here you are, Kara,' Bob said, bringing her a mug of coffee. He pulled another chair over.

'You're going to have a big hooley when your place is ready to move into, aren't you?' Bracken said.

'Hardly a hooley, Sean. More tea and cucumber sandwiches.'

The men looked at each other.

'Maybe some beer and wine, if you both behave

yourselves. I don't want you tossing your bag into a pot plant,' she said, sipping the coffee and looking over the rim at Bracken.

'That's disgusting, getting into a state like that,' Bob said, grinning.

'Listen to him. He's been poured into a taxi so many times, we've lost count.'

'Are we going to be losing you?' Bob asked.

'I'll have to move out sometime, Bob.' She smiled and put a hand on his. 'Don't worry, I won't be a stranger.'

He looked sad at the prospect of her going into her own house, like she was a daughter flying the coop. 'Got to go and help with the breakfasts,' he said, getting up from the table. 'Mary will have burnt the cornflakes by now.'

'Again, sexist bastard,' Bracken said. He shook his head and looked at Kara. 'Chaz had a note stuck on her windscreen last night at the mortuary when she was on the night shift,' he said.

'From who?'

'A dead man.'

'A dead man?' Kara looked puzzled.

'Howard Wilson.'

'Isn't that the man who was dead, but they thought he wasn't dead, but then he was dead?'

'The very same.'

'But he really was dead, wasn't he?' Kara said.

'He was. They don't mess about at the cremato-rium. Let's just say he was dead when they screwed the lid down.'

'Do you think a family member holds a grudge?'

'Or else it's the new guy down there, Jim Brown. They pranked him when he first started.'

'And now he's pranking her.'

'That's what I said to her.'

'Make sure she tells you if there're any more. Better to err on the side of caution.'

'I told her the same.' He stood up from the table. 'Going inside for breakfast?'

'I thought you were going to ask me for a dance again.'

'Never going to live that one down, am I?'

'Nope.'

SIX

'You look like a half-shut knife,' Jim Brown said to Terry Jones as he sat down at the table in their small break room, a coffee in one hand.

'What did you say?'

Brown laughed. 'I'm just kidding. No offence.'

'You need to watch your fucking mouth, son. You're on probation here, and from where I'm sitting, you're skating on thin ice.'

'Easy there, old-timer. I was just making a comment,' Brown said with a grin.

'Old-timer? I'll fucking knock you right out.'

'Jesus, get a grip. Can't you take a bit of banter?'

'Banter?' Jones said. 'Is that what you call it? Like putting a fucking note on Chaz's windscreen. Trying to put the shitters up her. Sick wee bastard. If I have anything to do with it, you won't last five more minutes here.'

'Me? Put a note on her windscreen? What are you talking about?' Any humour in Brown's voice was gone now.

'She told me about you creeping about in here late last night. Pretending to get a CD or some such shite. Watching Chaz, more like. Trying to frighten her. Well, we might have a laugh now and again, but we don't go about scaring lassies.'

'I did fuck all,' Brown said. He shot up from the table and pointed a finger at Jones. 'You get your facts straight before you start accusing me of anything.'

'It doesn't take a rocket scientist to figure it out, numb nuts: you were the only other one here! She caught you creeping about. Go on, admit it: you were here on your own when she came back from a run, weren't you?' Jones's voice had risen now and his eyes were wide.

'Well, yes, but...' Suddenly, the younger man didn't look so sure of himself.

'You know you're not allowed in here unless you're on duty? Because of victims of crime. You could be corrupt and bring some evidence in here or take it away. That's how they look at us. It's all protocol, and if you'd been paying attention at your fucking orientation, you would have known that!' Jones was raising his voice with every word.

'He's right, you know,' Dr Pamela Green said, coming into the room. The kettle had just gone off, so she poured herself a brew. 'You could get yourself in a lot of trouble, Jim. I need to report you to Professor Wall, who will want to take it further.'

'You need to, Dr Green,' Jones said. 'He was out of order. He should never have been here, and he knows it.'

'I was just getting a CD out of my locker,' Jim protested.

'You should know better,' Pamela said. 'You were told this at your training. Under no circumstances have you to be in the building unless you're on duty. You could have compromised a case or two.'

'I'm sorry, I didn't think,' Brown said.

'You're too busy clowning around and being a smartarse all the time. You think you're funny, but you're about as funny as a papercut on a tongue,' Jones said.

'Oh, shut up. Like you're perfect.'

'That's enough, both of you.' Pam looked at Brown. 'Let's get the first one done. We have a busy day ahead.'

Brown left and went to fetch Monica Lewis, one of the other attendants. The first guest of the day was Colin Paisley, who had been brought in first.

It didn't take long for the postmortem to be put on hold.

SEVEN

Myra Taylor looked up at the ceiling of the lab where she worked, as if the answer lay there. Then back at the machine sitting on the bench in front of her.

Angela Monroe hadn't answered any more texts after last night. Even knocking on her apartment door hadn't produced any results. She had thought about calling the police, just to go along and do a welfare check. But she didn't want to draw attention to herself.

'Everything okay?' William Potter said to her. The head of the lab stood beside her like an old schoolmaster checking on his pupil.

'Oh, yes. I was just wondering if Dr Monroe had

called in sick. We were supposed to be having lunch today and I haven't seen her.'

'She hasn't called in.'

'Maybe I should go down and see if she'll answer her door. I tried before, as usual, but there was no reply.'

'I know, you already told me that.' His tone was sharp.

'Don't get all freaky on me, Willie. If something's happened to her, I need to know.'

'What's wrong with you two recently?'

Myra thought about last night. About the fight with Beardy, how she could have gone berserk on him and probably killed him without breaking a sweat.

'Nothing.' She just smiled. Potter went out drinking with them, but in the lab it had to be all business. They weren't sure how the management would take a boss socialising with the lower members of staff.

Potter started walking away but stopped and stepped back towards Myra's bench. 'When you see Angela, tell her we need to have a little meet. Not showing up for work is not acceptable.'

'I know. It's not like her.'

'Just try to get hold of her, Myra,' Potter said in a softer voice.

EIGHT

Bracken put the phone down in his office and walked out into the incident room. 'Listen up. That was Angie Paton on the phone. She says hi and she's enjoying her training. And her promotion to DI, of course. Well deserved.'

Kara Page came into the incident room and they all looked at her. 'I heard what you said. That's good news. She's our loss but somebody else's gain. I hate to rain on the parade, but I got a call from Dr Green at the mortuary. She was doing the PM on a sudden death from last night. A young man from East Craigs found dead in his house. It's not a sudden death anymore.'

Bracken looked at DI Jimmy Sullivan. 'Let's go. The rest of you, carry on with what you were doing and I'll give you a call. Tam? Don't raid the biscuit tin.'

'As if, boss.'

The overweight Detective Sergeant Gale put on an exaggerated look of being offended. The older man had worked with another new team member, DC Lennox 'Doc' Docherty, on an undercover job months previously, and they had been asked to stay on in the MIT, having proven their worth.

'How's the diet going, boss?' Sullivan said as they made their way downstairs to the small car park at the back of the station.

'What do you mean, "diet"?' You been talking to Bob Long again?'

'I thought you said the biscuits were turning you into a fat bastard?'

'I said I would turn into a fat bastard if I kept on eating them. Cheeky bastard.' Bracken used the remote to open the doors on his Ford and Sullivan got in on the passenger side.

'My mistake,' the DI said.

'Do I look like I've put on weight or something?' Bracken started the car and booted it out into the lane behind the station, then joined the traffic and headed over to the Western Approach Road to hit Lothian Road.

'It's not that I notice,' Sullivan said, making a face.

'I've actually lost weight since I stopped eating shite. Bollocks to that working-out pish. Just watch your diet and walk up the stairs more often than taking the lift, that sort of crap.'

'If you say so.'

'I do say so. Fucking fat bastard indeed.' Bracken was sitting at traffic lights, waiting to turn left into Bread Street, taking the route that Chaz had taken with the van the night before. 'You were married before, Jimmy, weren't you? Didn't you tell me that?'

Sullivan looked out of the window for a moment. 'Did I tell you that?'

'To be honest, no. I overheard somebody talking to you about it one day.'

Sullivan turned to look at him. 'Earwigging? I thought you were above all that, boss.'

'Hardly earwigging, son. But I also don't have cloth ears.'

'Good point. But yes, I was married before.'

'You mind if I ask what went wrong?'

'I do actually,' Sullivan replied.

'Fair enough.' The light turned green and Bracken made the turn.

'We were young. It seemed like a good idea at the

time. It lasted six months before she left me for my best friend, who had been my best man. The best man won at the end of the day.'

'I didn't mean to poke into your business. You know I'm divorced.'

'Of course I do.'

'Ed and I met her new boyfriend last night. My ex invited us round for dinner and a few drams.'

'Oh aye? How did that go?'

'He's an okay bloke. How do they say it nowadays? He's slightly vertically challenged.'

'A midget?' Sullivan said.

'Fuck's sake. First of all, he's not that small. And second, they're not called that nowadays.'

'Saying "vertically challenged" implies that.'

'He's smaller than me. Smaller than my ex. And his hand is a lot smaller than mine. Or else I just have big hands.'

'You know what they say about a man with big hands,' Sullivan said with a grin.

'They wear big gloves?' Bracken shot him a sideways look.

'Aye, that's it. Big gloves. That's what you can say to Chaz on your honeymoon night: at least I wear big gloves.'

'I knew it was a mistake to talk about something serious with you.'

'I'm kidding, boss. You know you can talk to me about anything.'

'Shut your hole. I'm telling you fuck all from now on.'

Sullivan laughed as Bracken turned into the mortuary car park. Jim Brown let them in the staff door. Bracken looked at the younger man as if he wanted to punch him in the face. *Which it might come down to,* he thought.

'Detectives,' Brown said, sweeping his arm wide. Bracken looked at the arm, wondering if this would be the one that would be bent behind his back when he arrested him. Or had a wee chat with him.

'Chaz was busy last night. Twice. Two sudden deaths. One of which Dr Green wants to talk to you about. She and Professor Wall. She was working with him today.'

They stood in the receiving area, the smell of disinfectant hitting Bracken's nostrils. There was a room through the back where they kept the decomposing bodies, a fan sucking the fetid air out, but some of it lingered.

'Homeless guy,' Brown said, seeing the look on

Bracken's face. 'Poor bastard. But he's boggin' now. What's left of him. More soup than anything else.'

'If you're trying to make us vomit, we've seen and heard it all,' Sullivan said. Bracken could see that the colour in the DI's face had turned down a couple of notches.

'Would I do a thing like that?' Brown said with a grin. Now Bracken was picturing himself skipping the arresting part and going right for having a wee word with the bastard after hours. An image of a car battery and jump leads sprang into his mind.

'Is this wee toerag trying to wind you up?' Terry Jones said, walking across to them. He clapped a hand on Brown's shoulder, squeezing hard.

Brown slapped the hand away. 'Don't put your fucking hand on me like that, old bastard.'

Jones was older than Brown and a few years younger than Bracken, but he looked like one of those blokes who worked out before lying on a sunbed for five hours. Bracken thought the man should have known better, seeing as how he worked with death every day, but who was he to lecture? If the man wanted skin cancer, then so be it.

'What did you fucking call me?'

'You heard.'

'Did you hear about some deviant putting a note

on Chaz's windscreen in the wee hours?' Bracken said, watching the young man's face.

'Aye, I did. Who would do a thing like that?' Jones asked.

'She doesn't know, Terry. It put the wind up her.'

'I'll bet it did. Bastard. Don't worry, we'll keep an eye on her. And we'd better not find out it was you, Jim.'

'Piss off.'

'We'll get upstairs now,' Bracken said.

'Not taking the lift?' Sullivan said.

'You can if you want. Fat bastard,' Bracken said.

Sullivan laughed as they went through the door into the stairwell.

'What the hell is wrong with Terry these days?' Sullivan asked.

'I think it's called *a clash of personalities*.'

'It's going to be a big clash if they keep talking to each other like that.'

They went up to the next level, where the post-mortem suite was. Professor Simon Wall was in one of them with Dr Pamela Green. A young man was the guest of honour, lying with a sheet over him pulled up to just under his chin.

'Bracken!' Wall said. 'Sullivan! Glad you could

make it.' His face was like thunder and he looked like shite.

'You make it sound like Laurel and Hardy just entered the room,' Bracken said.

'Aw, come on,' Pamela said. 'Not those two. Starsky and Hutch I would have said.'

'That's it, get it out of your system.'

'Well, if you could stop gabbing like a pair of old women for a minute,' Wall said, 'we could get on with it.' He'd been off ill for a while, but now he was back with a vengeance. 'Come and have a look at this young man,' he snapped.

The detectives stood around the table, with the two pathologists flanking them. Wall pulled the sheet down a bit and they could see the very edge of the Y incision that had been made at the start of the PM.

'See the bruising on the neck?' Wall said.

Bracken looked at the bruising, then at Wall. 'And if I opened his eyelids, I'd see petechiae in his eyes.'

'Give the man a coconut.'

'Strangulation,' Sullivan said.

'Very good, Dr Watson,' Wall said. 'Hyoid is broken in the neck.'

'The attending doctor declared him life extinct,' Bracken said. 'He didn't notice the bruising?'

'Chaz said that there was an overturned chair in the man's living room, like he had maybe fallen over, and if the doctor just saw that, maybe he thought Colin here had hit the chair on his way down. It does happen, and then the cause of death is revealed to be murder when we get hold of them.'

'Right. I'll have two of my team come round as you finish off the PM.' It was protocol that two detectives be at the postmortem when it was a murder case, and as soon as it had become apparent that this was indeed a murder victim, the doctors had stopped immediately.

'Try to get them to be a bit more timely than you two. As much as you'd like to believe it, I don't actually spend my whole life in here,' Wall snarled at them and walked out.

Bracken looked at Pamela. 'He's not usually like this. What's eating him?'

'I have no idea. He's been like this for a couple of weeks now. He looks like crap. His eyes are red all the time, and he snaps at everybody. I've tried talking to him, but he just tells me to mind my own business.'

'Keep an eye on him, Pam.' Then to Sullivan:

'Get Tam round here. I'll call Izzie to meet me at the scene.' He turned to Pamela. 'Which was?'

'East Craigs. I have it written down.'

Bracken looked at Sullivan again. 'Get forensics to the scene too.'

NINE

The terraced house looked small as Bracken pulled up. The window in the front door had been repaired and there was no sign that anything traumatic had taken place the night before, except a latex glove that had been discarded by a paramedic.

Bracken knew Tam Gale would have something to say about going to the mortuary after having his lunch, but that was the way of it. He saw Izzie Khan waiting in a car for him.

He stepped out into the sunshine just as the forensics van turned into the dead-end street. Izzie got out of the car and walked over to him.

'I made the call. She's in there with her mother. Kim Gillespie, fiancée of Colin Paisley. They were due to be married next month. I read PC Ian

Ramage's report. He says that Kim was distraught when she came in.'

'Right, let's go and have a word.' Bracken looked at the forensics van as it pulled to a stop and went over to talk to the driver. 'Give us a few minutes before you come in. I want to interview the occupant. Then I'll get the mother to take her out of the house.'

'Very good, sir.'

Bracken walked up to Izzie and they approached the front door. An older woman answered, either the mother or Colin Paisley had been into older women.

'I'm Sharon Gillespie, Kim's mother. Come in. She's lying on the settee in the living room. She's gutted.' The mother looked to be in her fifties, with a weathered look about her.

She showed them through to where Kim had been lying on the couch, but now she was sitting up. Her hair was ruffled on one side and her eyes were red. A box of paper hankies was on the coffee table in front of the couch, with a large deposit of used ones in a wastebasket next to her.

'This is the police, love,' Sharon said. Kim looked at them like they were from another planet. Bracken showed her his warrant card.

'DCI Bracken. This is DS Khan.'

Kim looked blankly at them, as if they were a pair of clowns who had turned up a day early for the birthday party.

'We're here to talk about your boyfriend, Kim,' Izzie said. 'You don't mind if we call you Kim?'

'Of course she doesn't,' Sharon said. 'Do you, love?'

Kim looked at her mother and shook her head.

'Find a seat,' Sharon said, and Bracken looked at the choice of furniture, which was a recliner and a small dining table with two chairs at it. He looked at the chairs; they were wooden and looked reasonably heavy. One of them had been tipped over last night, apparently, and he could see why the uniform would think Colin had hit it when he fell.

'We're fine standing,' he said to her.

Bracken waited for Sharon to sit down, but she announced she would put the kettle on and scuttled out of the room. She was back a few seconds later, and Bracken wondered if she would be listening for the singing kettle or the click from the electric one.

'We have a few questions about last night,' Bracken began, then was halted as Sharon jumped in.

'My daughter's been through enough, Mr Bracken. Why would you want to dredge things up?'

'I'm sorry to have to tell you this, but Colin's death has been upgraded.'

'Upgraded?' Sharon said, anger zipping through her voice. 'Like what? Business class? The poor boy's dead. How can he be upgraded to anything?'

'Murder,' Bracken said simply.

They could hear Kim's breath catching. Sharon's mouth fell open, and for the first time, she was silent.

'Murder?' Kim said, her voice soft.

'That's right,' Izzie said. 'That's why we need to know where you were last night.'

Kim stared at the hanky box, as if she knew she wanted one but had lost all ability to grab one. Then she snatched one and held it to her face. 'Murdered?' she said again.

'She was with me,' Sharon said. 'Kim's a hair-dresser and she does work on the side. Going to people's houses. She was down at my place last night, giving me a little trim.'

Bracken thought the woman was going to ask him how it looked, and he bit back the answer of 'like you were dragged through a hedge backwards'.

'How was he murdered?' Sharon asked. Her tone was softer now, and although Bracken heard the kettle click, the woman made no move to go and make tea.

'I can't disclose that at the moment. The final postmortem is being carried out and the cause of death will be submitted later today, but the preliminary PM indicated murder.'

Kim wailed again and Sharon walked over to her daughter and sat on the arm of the couch. She put an arm around Kim.

'Have you any idea who would want to hurt Colin?' Bracken asked.

'No, none at all,' Kim said, tears spilling out of her eyes again. 'He was always having a laugh, and everybody who met him thought he was great fun. He never said a bad word against anybody.'

'Where did he work?'

'For the university pharmacology department as a researcher,' Kim said. She looked at her mother. 'Am I in danger?' Then the same question to Bracken.

'I don't know if this was some random attack or if Colin was targeted. For now, better err on the side of caution,' Bracken said.

'How well do you get on with your neighbours?' Izzie said.

Kim looked puzzled for a second. 'We all get on fine. Why do you ask?'

'The uniformed officer who found Colin had to

break in. The front door was locked. The call was made by one of the neighbours who was coming round for her Avon catalogue.'

'You don't think she did it, do you?' Sharon said.

'We'll be talking to her. Do you think she could be capable?' Bracken said.

'She's older than me,' Sharon said, 'so I highly doubt it.'

'Somebody was in here with Colin and they killed him, then they locked the door behind them. It wasn't deadbolted, but whoever came in had to have been let in. Or it was somebody with a key. Since your mother said you were at her house, we have to surmise that Colin let his killer in.'

The two women looked aghast.

'He let somebody in and that person killed him?' Kim said, her voice now a hoarse whisper.

'It's one theory we're working on,' Izzie said.

'Who would have murdered him?' Kim said, as if the detectives were about to draw names out of a hat.

'We need to find that out,' Bracken said. 'Now, we need to have a forensics team come in here and dust for fingerprints. I have to ask you not to touch anything else, especially those chairs.'

'Anything you need to do,' Kim said, dabbing at her eyes again.

Bracken said, 'What car do you drive? Both of you.'

'I have a Vauxhall Astra,' Sharon said.

'I have an Audi TT,' Kim replied. 'Colin bought it for me.'

'Do you have the names of people Colin worked with?' Bracken asked.

'I know some of their names, people he was closest to. Myra Taylor, Angela Monroe, William Potter. Those were his team members, the people he went out for a drink with on occasion. There are others too, but I can't recall their names.'

'Where is Colin's workplace located?' Izzie asked.

'Holyrood Road.' Kim gave them the exact location and Izzie wrote it down.

'Did Colin have friends outside of work?' Bracken asked.

'Of course he did,' Sharon said, taken on a defensive stance. 'He was a very pleasant man. You know the expression, *Wouldn't hurt a fly?*'

'Yes.'

'That wasn't him. Colin, unfortunately, liked a wee whisky to himself. Beer he was fine with, but the old hops would Jekyll and Hyde him. He lost quite a few friends that way. The night would start off fine, then he would start on the whiskies and then boom, he would be punching somebody. Of course, he wouldn't remember it in the morning, but that was even worse in my mind.'

'You think he might have got into a fight with somebody?' Izzie asked.

'Who knows? He might have annoyed somebody in the pub one night and they decided to get back at him,' Sharon said.

'We'll have somebody talk to the neighbours,' Bracken said. 'First, though, we have to get the forensics team in here.' He looked at Sharon. 'If you could give me your address, that would be great.'

She told Izzie, who wrote it down.

'We'll be in touch,' Bracken said, and they left the house. Outside, he instructed the forensics crew to move in.

'Sounds like our boy was a bit of a troublemaker,' Bracken said. 'Give you the shirt off his back indeed. More like, give you a punch in the mouth.'

'It happens to a lot of people,' Izzie said. 'Not me, of course; I don't drink.'

'Me neither.'

Izzie looked at him.

'Well, hardly anyway. Don't listen to Ed; he'll just make up stories about me.'

'I wouldn't dream of it, but your dad and I don't hang out much these days.' Izzie smiled; she had met Bracken's dad twice.

'Your life will be the better for it.'

'Oh, don't say that about him, sir. You would miss him if anything were to happen to him.'

'Aye, you're right.'

TEN

'You're sweatin' like a bastard there, Tam,' Sullivan said. 'You got malaria or something?'

'God, I ate a couple of mince pies before I came here. A little heads-up would have been nice. I think I'm going to toss my bag.'

'You've been to more PMs than I've had hot showers. An old hand like you should be used to this by now.'

'Less of the bloody old.' Gale took a hanky out of a pocket and dabbed his forehead. 'It fucking honks in here. Did they bring in a liquefied tramp again?'

'That's not very PC, Tam.'

'Nothing we say or do is right nowadays. My daughter chewed me out for not being "woke" the other night. Whatever the fuck that is. When I was younger, being "woke" was being shoogled awake by my mother when I was late for school.'

Sullivan laughed. They were in Pamela Green's office, drinking her coffee.

'I hope you two put a couple of shillings in the coffee jar,' Pamela said as she came in and sat behind her desk.

'What's a shilling?' Gale asked.

'You know fine well what a shilling is, Tam Gale. You've been round the block more than once, so don't give me that.'

'Listen, Doc, I'm turning fifty next month, not a hundred and fifty. Which reminds me, you coming to my party?'

She looked at him. 'I didn't get an invite.'

'I haven't sent them out yet.'

'Of course we'll be there. My husband is always up for a party.'

'Terrific. I'm thinking of having it in the police club. It'll be fun, like having a secret ball.'

'You made that sound like there's something wrong with you,' Sullivan said. 'Secret ball.'

'You know what I mean. It'll be fun. A Saturday night with all the gang there.'

'Just get it booked early, Tam. I wouldn't want to mark my calendar and then be disappointed,' Pamela said. 'It'll be the social event of the year.'

'Mock if you must, Dr Green, but we'll be having a good time.'

'I'm not mocking, Tam. My kids are teenagers now, but there were years where we had to forego any parties because of the kids. I'm genuinely looking forward to it.'

Gale nudged Sullivan in the ribs. 'See that? Even the good doctor is looking forward to it. Best get your babysitter booked up now, Jimmy boy. I promise that when you wake up the following morning, you won't even remember having been out. A good time will be had by all.'

'Been a long time since I was at a party like that.'

'Me too.'

Just then, Professor Wall came along the corridor and stopped at Pamela's office. 'I'm glad you two are still here,' he said, slightly out of breath. Sullivan knew the man jogged, and yet here he was, out of breath. Jogging? The man was hardly the poster boy for getting healthy.

'The PM was just completed on Colin Paisley,' Sullivan told him.

'I need you to attend the one I've started.'

'Why? What's wrong?' Gale asked.

'We have another murder victim. It would seem Dr Angela Monroe was killed in the same way as Mr Paisley.'

ELEVEN

Chaz Cullen hated working nights. When she got home, she was usually wired; that was why she called Bracken over, thinking that maybe him making love to her would tire her out and she would sleep right through until it was time to get up and make something to eat. The last time she was on nights, Bracken had come round in the evening and had left when she left for work.

The overnights were just one more reason she was considering leaving this job and going to the nine-to-five. Better hours. More pay. So what was stopping her?

Nothing.

Not anything she could think of. Except maybe she would get bored being under the same roof all day. That was one of the things she and Bracken had discussed. Right now, she got to go out and about to crime scenes. Drive the van on nights. Interact with different people all the time. She had made friends in the police force, especially Bracken, whom she was attracted to right off the bat. He was thirteen years older than she was, and some people might find that creepy, but love was what it was.

Of course, the pay would be better in the lab. She would go right in as an advanced biomedical scientist, utilising her degree. It was a win-win. But it was a big change.

She lay in bed, trying to get back to sleep. A colleague had told her to drink a couple of cans of lager when she got home after the night shift and that would knock her out, and it worked. But something had woken her and she was trying to get back to sleep to no avail.

Then she got up to use the bathroom, and saw the pile of mail on the floor. It had been the postie putting the mail through the door that had woken her. She padded along the hallway in her bare feet and picked it up. She could have left it, of course, but curiosity got the better of her. Maybe in the pile of bills and junk mail there would be a surprise. A letter telling her that a long-lost uncle had passed on and left her his fortune.

Nah, that wouldn't happen.

But there *was* a card. She took the mail through to the living room and put the rest down on the coffee table. A flyer for new windows, one for a lawn company to come and give her better-looking grass (maybe they could help her with the house plants, to stop her killing every one that came into the house) and a brown envelope with some kind of bill tucked away inside, waiting to pounce when she opened it.

Her name and address had been printed out onto a label and stuck on the front of the light-blue card envelope. Maybe some more marketing crap?

There was no return address on it.

She ran a finger under the flap, careful not to give herself a paper cut. Flap open, she gripped the card with finger and thumb and pulled it out.

On the front was a picture of a bouquet of flowers in muted colours, with the word *Condolences* written in gold across it.

Her heart beating faster, she slowly opened the card and her eyes went to the printed words first.

So sorry for your loss.

Then the handwritten words, written in black ink below the printed words.

I'm so sorry to hear about the passing of Sean. I know he was a special person in your life and his death has hit everybody so hard. He will be sorely missed by everybody.

Howard

TWELVE

Bracken was about to ask the old professor if he was sure but caught himself in time.

Sullivan had called him and updated him on the situation.

'Petechiae in the eyes?' he asked instead.

Sullivan and Gale stood on the other side of the steel table, looking down at the corpse of Angela Monroe.

'It wasn't noticed before because she was brought in by that girl. The doctor at the scene once again said it looked like a fall.'

'By that girl, you mean Chaz?' Bracken said, his voice clicking up a notch. The old bastard had already gone into self-preservation mode.

'Yes, the one with the blue streak in her hair. I hope she's professional enough for this job.'

'The blue streak is gone now, Doc,' Bracken said. *If you cleaned your fucking glasses occasionally, you would know that.*

'Aye, well, still.'

'She's not a pathologist,' Bracken countered, feeling his hackles rise.

'If she's been here for a while, she would start to see things that the untrained eye wouldn't. Like the petechiae. Maybe it's better if she does decide to leave. I don't think her head's in the game anymore.' Wall shook his head. 'Good God. Young people nowadays. I mean, look: there's bruising on the neck. What does that say about the force doctor who was called out?'

'That he's a doctor and not a pathologist.'

'He should expect to look at the deceased and have an educated guess.'

'Wasn't she found in the Queen's Park?' Tam Gale said. 'Where it was dark, poorly lit and out in the open.'

'And?' Wall said. 'I won't accept excuses for shoddy work. He should have had a torch and that would have clearly shown the bruising.'

'Like the one on her arm?' Bracken said, pointing. 'Or the one on her face? Or her forehead? I mean, if he had lifted up her clothing, he might have seen the bruising on her chest. Or there on her legs.'

'What are you implying?' Wall said, all signs of 'Welcome to the club' now gone. It was definitely *them or us*, and Wall wasn't going down without a fight.

'I'm not *implying* anything. I'm *inferring* that the bruising on her person would indicate a fall, and considering the location where she was found, that was a reasonable assumption. I mean, when you saw the bruising and knew where she had been found, did you think it was a fall or murder?' Bracken asked, his voice rising an octave or two.

'I don't take anything for granted in my job. But if I had been first at the scene and seen the bruising on her neck, I would have thought about it and questioned it. Cullen should have spotted it as well. She's been at enough crime scenes.'

'Maybe if she was paid big bucks like you, Doctor, she would have. She's a mortuary assistant, and a damned fine one at that. Her job is to bring in the dead, and I believe she did that perfectly. Your job is to discover whether somebody was murdered.

Which you have. You both did what you are paid for. There's no problem here.'

Wall shook his head and tutted. Then he looked closer at the corpse.

Terry Jones came into the room. Wall looked up at him. 'Jones. You cleaned this woman, didn't you?'

'Yes, sir. I cleaned her. She was dirty from the fall.'

'Her hair has been brushed backwards. I didn't recognise her at first, but now I do. Angela Monroe. *Dr* Angela Monroe. She works down at the university's pharmacology unit. Literally five minutes from us. Good God. Who would want to murder her?'

Nobody had the answer.

When Bracken was downstairs, he bumped into a young man he had known before he had left for Fife. An undertaker.

'Marcus King. How are you doing? It's been a long time,' Bracken said.

'DCI Bracken. It most certainly has. How have you been?'

They shook hands.

'Working hard. You know how it is. Death creates a lot of misery, but it also creates a lot of money – am I right?' Bracken said.

'You certainly are. Listen, I have to get off now, but maybe we can catch up for a beer sometime.'

'I'd like that,' Bracken said. He had no intention of drinking with the man, but it was good to see him again.

THIRTEEN

Myra Taylor told William Potter that she was going to have a late lunch. She had a feeling in the pit of her stomach that something was wrong. Angela was never late, would never have left it so long to talk to her throughout the day, even if she *had* been pished the night before.

She walked down Holyrood Road from the university. She and Angela never spent more than a day apart. Working in the lab was great: the money was good, the uni put them up in quality rental apartments, they each had a car that was leased by the uni. It was a great money-making game.

She looked around her, thinking of her fight with Beardy last night. She walked past the modern grey edifice of Unite Students accommodation at Sugar-house Close. This whole area had changed over the years. Edinburgh on the whole was shedding its skin to take on a whole new persona.

She thought about nipping into the Tesco Extra to grab a sandwich but dismissed the idea. Now she was speed-walking, looking at strangers to see if any of them were following her. None were, so far as she could tell.

She finally reached their apartment block and turned into Hutton Road, where the entrance door was. She took her keys out and got into the lift. A man in a black suit got in beside her.

They took it to the third floor, and Myra went one way, while the man went to Angela's door.

Myra went inside her own apartment and looked out through the peephole, just in time to see the man go inside.

She kept watching, and after a few minutes, she saw him come out of the apartment, this time with a holdall. Then he left the way he had come.

FOURTEEN

'Did you hear that cheeky bastard?' Bracken said as he and Sullivan got into the car. DC Docherty had turned up to observe the PM with Tam Gale, freeing up Sullivan.

'He's just a cranky old man,' Sullivan said, pulling his seat belt as Bracken shot the car out of the mortuary car park.

'Cranky my arse. He's only in his fifties. Don't try to make excuses for him. He's covering his own arse. She should have been checked over first thing. I mean, you saw the state the deceased was in. How was Chaz supposed to notice in the dark? And the force doctor is going to get a verbal from me when I get hold of him.'

'I don't blame you for being angry at him.'

'Stop making excuses for them, Jimmy. I hate this closing ranks pish.'

They went through the lights and Bracken saw the lane on the left for the university. They had been told to look for a boarded-up church on the corner, and here they were. Bracken parked the car in St John Street, and they went in through the modern building at the side and were asked to go to the reception.

'DCI Bracken. DI Sullivan. We're here to talk to somebody here about one of your staff members, Dr Angela Monroe.'

'Oh, right. I'll have her boss come and see you,' the woman said, and she turned away, picking up a telephone.

'I don't think they get many visitors here,' Sullivan said. 'No couches, no dog-eared magazines carrying some unknown disease.'

'I wonder how many visits from the polis they get?'

A door opened on the left and a man appeared. 'Good afternoon. I'm Professor William Potter. I believe you want to speak to me about Dr Monroe?'

He looked at them through fashionable glasses, and his eyes flitted between the two detectives.

'Somewhere private,' Bracken said, after introducing them again.

'Certainly. Through here.'

Potter held the door for them and they walked through, then stopped to wait for him.

They followed him down a corridor and he led them into an office. They sat down and Potter looked at them.

'Is everything alright with Angela? She didn't show up for work today.'

'Sorry to have to tell you this, but she's dead,' Bracken said.

Both Bracken and Sullivan heard the breath catch in Potter's throat and he sat back in his chair as if one of them had smacked him. 'Dead?' he said, his voice now dry and cracked as if all the fluid had left him.

'We need more information about her. I believe she wasn't married?'

Potter nodded. 'Correct.'

'Any next of kin that you know of?'

Potter lowered his head and looked at his desk as if the answer lay there.

'A mother, I think. She lives in Orkney. Angela didn't have a boyfriend that I know of.'

'We've made a formal identification because she

was known to one of the pathologists, but we don't have an address for her. She was identified with a university ID card.'

'She lives down the road in a rented apartment. I'll look up the address that we have on file for you.' Potter poked at the keys on his keyboard and the laser printer on a side table whirred. He stood up and passed the sheet of paper to them. 'It's a relatively new building called The Park. Presumably because it's near the Queen's Park. I can't imagine what they would have called it if it had been built near a waste transfer station.'

'We're here because Dr Monroe was murdered. Do you know of anybody who would want to harm her?' Bracken asked.

'Murdered?' Potter took a few deep breaths and started hyperventilating. The detectives stood up and Bracken went round to him.

'Take it easy. Slow your breathing a bit.' He put a hand on the man's back, wishing he had paid more attention at the advanced medical training course.

Potter slowly relaxed. Sullivan was on his feet, holding his phone, preparing to either make a phone call or run to get somebody. Either way, he was standing like a lemon, not sure what he should be doing.

Bracken nodded for him to sit down and went back round the desk to join him.

Potter had settled, but his face had paled.

'Murdered?' he said again, and Bracken wondered if now was the time to drop the fact that Colin Paisley was in the same boat.

'I'm afraid so. Did Angela have any enemies here?'

'What? Enemies? No, of course not. We have very tight-knit teams.'

'What did she do here?'

'I can only tell you the basics. We work on government contracts here and are subject to secrecy laws, but I can tell you, she worked in a lab. You see that old church at the front of our building? That's the lab. It looks like an old church because that's exactly what it is. The inside has some state-of-the-art lab facilities, but people walk by and don't give it another thought. It's accessed through a tunnel that links both buildings.'

'Can I ask what she was working on?'

'You can ask, Chief Inspector, but I can't tell you.'

Bracken looked at the man. *In for a penny*, he thought. 'Did she work with Colin Paisley?'

Potter nodded. 'He's on her team.'

'He was also murdered last night. You see, Professor Potter, when we investigate murders, we look for a connection, trying to join the dots together. There's our connection right there: two people work together, two people are murdered. On the same day. Do you know if either of them had any problems outside of work?'

'Colin murdered? Good God. I don't believe it,' Potter said. He took a few seconds to gather his thoughts before looking Bracken in the eyes. 'Problems? I don't think so.'

Bracken opened his hands as if in prayer. 'Like some people have gambling debts. They owe a lot of money to some bad people and those people decide to harm them for not paying. That sort of thing.'

'You think they both had gambling debts?'

'No, that was just an example.' *Fuck's sake.* 'Anything like that? Where people might want to harm them?'

'No. They worked in a lab and they lived quiet lives, as far as I can tell. But you never truly know people, do you? I mean, Colin might have been a closet psychopath for all we know. Your colleague there, he could be a cross-dresser without you knowing it.'

Bracken looked at Sullivan, whose cheeks were starting to take on a reddish hue.

'You couldn't have said, "He might be a member of a secret underground fight club," no?'

'That was just an example. By looking at you, I didn't think you could fight your way through a wet newspaper.'

Bracken looked at Potter. 'Best not put that to the test, though. So that's a no to Colin Paisley running with a bad crowd?'

'Colin was very friendly. He was always smiling and had a joke for everybody.'

'He liked to go boxing when he was full of the whisky, so we heard.'

'It grabbed him like that, yes. Pleasant bloke one minute; racist, sexist pig after the whisky went past his lips. Not a very good fighter, but he tried nonetheless, fuelled by the drink.'

'Can we have a look in the lab?' Bracken said, sure that Sullivan would be anxious to get away from the cross-dressing slur.

'No, that's not possible. You would have to get a warrant, and even then, it would have to be run through the government, and they wouldn't let anybody in. The work we do is classified. Nobody's going to let you in there.'

'Fair enough. We don't want to step on anybody's toes.' They stood up and Bracken took out a business card and passed it to Potter. 'If you can think of anything, please get in touch.'

'I will.' He remained seated. 'You know the way out.'

Bracken nodded, and he and Sullivan made their way out.

'He's trusting,' Sullivan said. 'We could just go wandering about.'

'Jimmy, he scoffed at the thought of you fighting illegally; I'm sure he's not worried about the prospect of us snooping. There are cameras everywhere. Bet you a pound the only door that's unlocked right now is the one leading out.'

Bracken was right. They made it out into the sunshine, with a little wind blowing up the narrow street.

'A secret government lab in that scabby old church?' Sullivan said. 'Who knew? It's all a bit James Bond, if you ask me.'

'Let's go down and have a look at Angela's apartment. I asked Docherty to meet us there with the warrant. He sent me a text saying he's there already.'

'That laddie's got his heid on straight. Even Tam Gale isn't as annoying as I thought he would be.'

'Don't tell him you think that. He might ask you outside for a fight, not knowing your reputation as a street boxer. As long as you don't get cross with him. Get it?'

'Oh, bog off.'

FIFTEEN

'This is it,' Sullivan said. 'Third floor.'

'What gave it away? The wee light that says number three on it? Or the doors opening?'

'If I really was a secret bare-knuckle boxer, you think I'd stand for this all the time?'

'Of course you would,' Bracken said, stepping out of the lift and turning left. 'Because you know what I would do to you if you lifted your hand to me.'

'That kind of talk might scare some wee lassie, but I'm younger, fitter and have more stamina.'

Bracken turned quickly and poked Sullivan in the guts with his thumb. Sullivan gasped.

'Jesus, I wasn't prepared then.'

'You won't be prepared when I come after you.'

'Jesus, boss, I was only kidding. About smacking you one. Of course I show respect –'

'If you say "to your elders", I swear you'll be going back down in the lift shaft without the aid of the lift.'

'I wouldn't dream of it.' Sullivan took the key from his pocket, the one given to them by Paul downstairs in the lobby.

'Where's Heid-the-Baw with the warrant?' Bracken asked.

The stair door banged open further along. 'Talk of the Devil.' Bracken looked at DC Lennox Docherty, wheezing and gasping as he half-ran, half-stopped himself from puking.

'Jesus, Doc, you look like you've been licking windows again. Your shirt's half-out and you're sweating like he was earlier. I'm sure you pair have got malaria.'

'I was running, sir. You told me to hurry.'

'You can't go in the lift?' Bracken was still incredulous about this fact.

'It's an illness,' Sullivan confirmed.

'You seem to manage just fine,' Bracken said. 'You could do with losing some weight. My thumb went into your gut to the first knuckle.'

'What? Away. Bloody wall of steel, that.'

'Ball of bloody wool, more like.'

'Aye, well, let's get this door open. I want to see if there's any sign that Angela Monroe was murdered here.'

Bracken took the key, unlocked the door and gently pushed it in. There was no immediate smell and they walked in with caution. Bracken had heard of a murderer staying in his victim's house for days, but if there was somebody here, he would be taking on three grown men, one of whom was big and, according to Sullivan, had big hands.

The apartment was empty and there was no obvious sign that a struggle had gone on in here. That didn't mean there *hadn't* been a struggle, but if there had been, the killer had done a good job of clearing up.

Plus, if Angela *had* been murdered here, there would have been some signs left from her body. But there was nothing.

Still, it wouldn't do any harm to get the forensics crew in.

'Doc, get a uniform crew in here to stand guard. I don't want anybody else coming in here until forensics gets done with it.'

'Yes, sir.' Docherty walked away to another room to make the call.

'Maybe she was just out for a walk and somebody killed her in the park,' Sullivan said.

Bracken was looking out of the window into the courtyard below. The building was in a U shape, surrounding the communal gardens, hidden behind a wall from the public. He could see part of the tented roof of Our Dynamic Earth in the distance. It was a nice apartment.

Docherty came back into the room. 'I made the call, sir. There's a patrol round the corner. They'll be here in two minutes.' He was holding a fist out to Bracken, fingers up. 'I also found this on the floor.'

He turned his hand round, waiting for Bracken to hold out a hand. The DCI obliged.

Docherty dropped a little blue pill into his hand. Bracken looked at him. 'Are you trying to be funny, son?'

'What?'

Sullivan smiled. 'He's not that far aged that he needs a wee blue pill.'

'Oh, no. I don't think it's Viagra,' Docherty said.

'What makes you think it isn't?' Bracken asked the younger detective.

'I think Viagra is four-sided. The official one, not the knock-off. Isn't it?' Docherty said, looking at Sullivan.

'Why are you looking at me? I'm married with two kids.'

'Tiredness gives you the droop. Not to mention brewer's droop,' Bracken offered.

'Again, why me? I'm thirty-five.' The two younger detectives looked at Bracken.

'Shut your hole, both of you, and get the bloody thing in a plastic evidence bag,' he replied, holding his hand out for Docherty to put the pill into the bag that had appeared from his pocket.

There was a knock at the door and the three men stood looking from the living room to the small hall-way. The door was off to the right.

'Well, don't just stand there, Docherty, go and answer the bloody thing. And if you see a couple of thin pipes being poked through the letterbox, it's probably not the plumber.'

'Oh, God,' Docherty said, but walked through into the hall cautiously. There were no pipes being put through the letterbox because there wasn't one. Residents had a mailbox downstairs. He put his eye to the peephole, thinking that if there was somebody with a shotgun on the other side, then he could be waiting for the peephole to go dark before pulling the trigger.

He kept his eye there for a second and saw a

woman. He grabbed the door handle and yanked the door open.

The woman screamed and then launched herself at Docherty. She grabbed an arm and then tripped him, but before she could rearrange his jaw, Bracken stepped in and grabbed her arm.

She looked up at him, trying to pull her arm away, but Sullivan was round, helping Bracken while Docherty scooted out from under the melee.

'Get your hands off me!' Myra Taylor shouted.

Bracken handcuffed her. 'You're under arrest for assaulting a police officer,' he said.

Then the air fell out of Myra. She had been pushed up against the wall. 'Police?' she said. 'I thought he was a friend of the guy who attacked us last night.'

Bracken turned her around. 'What's your name?'

'Myra Taylor. I'm a friend of Angela's. We were accosted last night and I fought him off while Angela ran. I thought his friend was here.'

'Close the door,' Bracken ordered Docherty. 'Wait for the uniforms. On the other side.' Bracken ushered her through to the living room while Docherty let himself out, and Sullivan followed Bracken.

'I'm going to take the cuffs off, and I want you to

sit down and tell me what happened, okay? I want you to show me some ID. Understand?'

'Yes, of course. You first.'

Both Bracken and Sullivan brought their warrant cards out and showed them to her before Bracken took the cuffs off. Myra showed them her driving licence.

She was sitting on the couch, facing the large TV, and Bracken sat in a chair that was positioned nearest the door. Sullivan had already put himself there, so if this woman wanted to escape, that only left the door out onto the balcony. Three floors up from the courtyard.

Myra didn't show any inclination that she wanted to run.

'You have the floor, Ms Taylor.'

'I live next door. Angela and I are friends as well as workmates. I sent her a text last night, and she was fine. I usually knock on the door when it's time to go to work. We work just up the road at the university. There was no answer this morning, so I went to work myself.'

'Is it unusual for her not to answer the door?' Bracken said.

'Yes. I sent her a text, telling her to call me later. I thought the drink we'd had last night had knocked her out.' She looked puzzled, as if a thought had just hit her. 'Why are you in here? Was she arrested or something?'

Bracken was silent for a moment before answering. 'I'm sorry to tell you that Angela was found dead this morning.'

Myra sucked in a breath like the room was suddenly devoid of air. Then the words rushed out like a steam train. 'Died? How did she die? In here? Or was it outside? Who found her? How did she die? Where did she die? Could I have let myself in and helped her?'

Bracken put up a hand. 'She was found dead in the Queen's Park.'

Myra was silent for a moment. 'Queen's Park?' Like this was so farfetched it couldn't even be true.

'I'm afraid so. She was murdered.'

Myra sat and stared at Bracken for what felt like hours. 'Murdered? Angela? How could that be? She was home. She sent me a text.'

'Can I see your phone? Show me the text.'

Myra opened up the page of texts and showed Bracken the one she'd been sent by her friend the night before.

He nodded and she took it back.

'How did she end up in the park?' Myra asked.

'We don't know. We were hoping her friends could help us.'

'She wouldn't go there after dark.'

'It was the summer solstice last night,' Sullivan said. 'It would have been light till late, then light early again. Do you think she could have gone there to watch the sunrise? Some people do.'

'If she was interested in that, she would have said.'

'Tell us about the man who accosted you last night,' Bracken said.

Myra took a deep breath and let it out before speaking. 'We were in the pub and this weirdo was looking over at us, so I went over to him and asked him to stop. He made a nasty comment, but then he left. We were taking a shortcut through one of the closes when we heard somebody coming up behind us. It was Beardy. He tried to punch Angela, but I stepped in and smacked him around a bit. I told Angela to run, and she did. When I'd taken care of Beardy, I texted her and she said she was home.'

'What about Beardy?' Sullivan asked. 'Where did you leave him?'

'In the close. He was down but not out. I thought he would start chasing me again, but I would have given him a good belting.' She looked between the two detectives. 'I used to do kick-boxing.'

Bracken believed it. One on one, she would give any man a run for his money. But what she had in finesse, he had in sheer size and power.

'Do you think he could have followed you?' Bracken asked, keeping his hands in front of himself. Just in case.

'I didn't think so. I slapped him about, but he might have recovered quickly.'

'Could you describe him to a sketch artist?' Sullivan asked.

'I can do better than that.' She took her phone out and opened the photos on it and showed Bracken. 'I'll AirDrop it to you.'

Bracken looked at the man's bleeding face. 'Okay. Go ahead.' After a couple of minutes, it was there on his phone.

'There's no way he could have got to Angela?' Bracken said.

'No chance. She was way ahead of him, and he would have had to get past me, which he didn't.'

'He might have filed a report on being assaulted,' Bracken said. 'In which case, we might have to talk again on that subject. Defending yourself means you can go one step above the level of force used by your attacker.'

'That's shite and you know it. Legal mumbo jumbo. If somebody comes at you, do what you need to do to stop the bastard. I would rather be judged by a jury than carried by a funeral director.'

Bracken knew she had a point, and he agreed with it, but officially, he had to tell her that the law wasn't on her side. Like most cases these days, where a slap on the wrist for violent offenders seemed to be the norm. He had told his own daughter, Sarah, the same thing: do what you need to do to get away. It's your life or theirs.

'How well do you know Colin Paisley?' Sullivan asked.

Myra snapped her head round to look at him. 'Colin? I work with him. Why?'

'He's dead,' Bracken said. Now Myra looked at him. 'What? Colin?'

'Yes, Colin. He was murdered in the same way as Angela,' Bracken told her.

Myra's mouth opened and closed a couple of times as if she was a goldfish looking out of her bowl. Her piercing blue eyes bore into his and he could see her body tense.

'I don't believe it. Why would anybody want to murder Colin?' she asked.

'That's what we're trying to find out.' He didn't take his eyes off her.

'Kim is going to be devastated.'

'I spoke to Kim and her mother,' Bracken said. 'Kim is beside herself.'

'I can imagine. She loved Colin more than anything. They were planning to move into a bigger house after the wedding.'

'Do you live alone?' Sullivan asked.

'Yes. Why?' Her eyes were focused on him now. The shock of hearing about Colin's death had seemingly passed.

'I just wanted to know if you could verify you were here alone last night after your little rough and tumble with Beardy.'

'Well, I can't. I came home, had a shower and went to bed.'

'There are security cameras in the lobby that can confirm that.'

'Please check them. You'll see I'm telling the truth.'

Bracken stood up. 'We'll be in touch. Meantime, if you can think of anything else...' He handed her a

business card and waited until she had left Angela's
flat. Myra gave Docherty a dirty look as she left.

'You think she killed her workmates?' Sullivan
asked.

'My gut says no, but I want somebody to go
round to the pub they were in and talk to whoever
was on last night. See what time they left.'

'I'll get on it.'

'The uniforms are here,' Docherty said, coming
into the apartment now that Myra was away.

'Get a door-to-door going in here. I want to know
if anybody saw or heard anything.'

Docherty nodded, then Bracken left, leaving
Sullivan with the younger detective. In the lobby,
Paul was on duty.

'Can you look up footage on the CCTV system
from last night?'

'Sure. No problem. Come back into our wee
office.'

Paul led the way and Bracken saw the monitor
with a view of the reception area.

'Eleven o'clock onwards,' Bracken said, and Paul
obliged. He scrolled through hours, but nobody
came in.

'Myra Taylor said she was home. Would she
have come in here through the lobby?'

'Not if she went into the parking garage under-neath the building. There are no working cameras there. They're knackered, and getting the homeown-ers' association to get anything done is like pulling teeth. She could have got in the lift and taken it up to her floor, but –'

'The cameras are knackered in the lift too.'

'Correct.'

'Okay, thanks.'

SIXTEEN

'You look tired, Sean. You getting enough sleep?'

'No.' Bracken looked at Kara Page as they stood in the driveway of what had once been an immaculate house. The petrol and box of matches had taken care of it, and it had been a toss-up whether she wanted to take the insurance money and run or use it to rebuild.

'How about you?' he said to her. 'I hope you don't mind me saying, but maybe a couple of wee teabags on your eyes might give them a lift.'

'I do mind, cheeky bugger. Nothing wrong with my eyes.'

They stood looking at the scaffolding on the house. The builders were long gone for the day. The landscaping would be taken care of after all the construction equipment was gone. Right now, it looked like what it was: a building site.

'I've decided I'm going to sell,' she said, digging her hands into her lightweight jacket. It was the middle of summer, but there was always a wind coming across the field behind the house.

'Where will you go?'

'I'll stay at the guest house until I find the right place. Just like you.'

'Bob and Mary are lifesavers. I mean, each property I've gone for, I've been outbid on.'

'Have you thought about renting?'

Bracken was silent for a moment. The dwindling sunlight caught the new windows as it slowly finished its dance for the day. 'Aye, I have. But I think in the back of my mind, I don't want to leave until my dad gets settled back in his own home.'

'Have the insurance paid out on his house?'

Bracken's father had lived in a mobile home in Fife until a psycho had torched it, just like somebody had torched Kara's house.

'They have, but the new ones cost a lot more. He's short right now.'

'He's comfortable being in the little room at the top of the guest house with Max, though, isn't he?'

'He is. He pays his way, of course, but Bob and

Mary cut him a deal because he helps out around the house. They hate taking money from him, but he insists.'

'He keeps beating me at poker. He's had a tidy sum out of me.'

'Beats you, Kara, or you let him win?' Bracken smiled.

'Actually, I was lenient with him a bit at first, but he really is a good player. It's pride that keeps me going. I want to win some of my money back.'

'Talk of the Devil,' Bracken said as Ed came round from the back of the house with Max.

'Sorry about that, Kara, but Max was needing to pee,' Ed said, and the dog pulled him across the driveway like he hadn't seen Kara or Bracken for weeks.

'Easy, pal,' Bracken said as Max shoved his head between Bracken's legs. Bracken patted the dog on the back and rubbed his side.

'It's looking good round there,' Ed said. 'Are you going to miss it?'

Kara shook her head. 'We weren't in it for long before I got transferred to Inverness. It only had tenants in it after that. Tony and I didn't make any memories in there. None to write home about anyway.'

'You could tell some stories about the guest house, what with Barbara Woodhouse there,' Bracken said.

'Hush your cake hole. Comparing me to a woman.'

'You are an old woman at times. No wonder Kara is pulling the wallpaper off in her room.'

'Don't listen to him, Ed,' Kara said, laughing. Max gave her attention now.

'Right, that's enough, pal,' Ed said to his dog, gently tugging on the lead. Max left her and stood beside his master.

'Two murders on the same day,' Kara said, 'and they worked with each other. Not a coincidence.'

'No. Not at all. We're looking into their backgrounds, but nothing is jumping out. Neither had a criminal record; people talk highly of them. If it was just Angela, I might have said she'd been a victim of an attempted mugging, but when you factor in her friend texting her and Angela replying she was at home, then that blows it out of the water.'

'I agree. My best guess is, somebody took her to the park, either by force or coaxing her to go. Then they took her phone and sent the text to Myra Taylor, pretending to be Angela.'

'That sounds right,' Bracken said. 'Also, we

found a little blue pill in Angela's bedroom. I thought it was Viagra, but Docherty seems to think it's something different.' Bracken looked at Ed. 'Let's ask the expert.'

'Oh, shut up. I don't need that stuff,' Ed said, making a face.

'Relax, Dad, I'm kidding. I mean, you're too old for shenanigans anyway.'

'Look who's talking.'

'I have a girlfriend, remember.'

'The lab will run it and give you a definitive answer,' Kara said. 'Don't make any bets with your dad. He's got a good poker face.'

Ed grinned. Then his face fell and Max perked up. 'Don't look now, here's Fuzz Face.'

Both Kara and Bracken turned to see the neighbour from across the road stomping towards them.

'Do you know him?' Bracken asked his dad.

'Of course not. Did you think Fuzz Face was his first or last name?' Ed shook his head.

'Oh, I see: you have a nickname for everybody.'

'Aye. Baldy, the guy who lives next door to us. Heid-the-Baw, that lanky streak of piss on the other side. The one who thought Max was pissing on his flowers. Numb nuts, who lives a few doors along.'

'That's the church. You call the minister numb nuts?'

'Before the church, dafty.'

'Oh God, it's him again,' Kara said in a low voice. She looked at Bracken. 'Now you see why I'm selling.'

'Mrs Page!' The man was waving an arm about like she couldn't see him.

'It's Miss Page, actually,' she said as he got closer.

Max started barking and Ed started chuckling.

'I'd appreciate it if you would keep the Hound of the Baskervilles under control,' he said.

This man lived directly across the road in a large, detached house. It seemed that none of the neighbours were very happy to see Kara move into her house.

'Call him that again, baw bag, and I'll let him loose. He sees you as a threat. Must be the bushy beard and the seventies glasses. You want to get yourself a mirror in your house, chum,' Ed said, tugging on Max's collar. The dog settled with just a low growl in his throat.

'That dog touches me and I'll have it put down,' the man said.

'Technically, you're trespassing. The dog has a right to guard the property since I invited him onto it, but I haven't invited you,' Kara said. 'Now, you seem to be at an advantage.' She waited for him to introduce himself, but he didn't.

'I want to complain about all the noise that's been going on. Those builders make a noise from early in the morning, all day until five o'clock. My wife's sick of it. What are you going to do about it?'

'They're in compliance, so I'm not going to do anything about it.'

'Well, that's awkward. Here I am, trying to tell you to shut those men up, and here you are, showing complete disregard.'

'They're almost done with the house.'

'Not good enough.'

'What do you suggest I do? Just get them to leave it like it is?'

'Tell them to be quiet!' he said, pointing a finger at Kara and taking a step forward. Max was having none of it and leaped up, straining against his lead, snarling and barking.

The man jumped back but gritted his teeth. 'This isn't over!' He turned and walked away, then stopped when he was at a distance. 'I hope somebody else burns it down.'

'That could be construed as a threat in front of witnesses,' Bracken said.

'It could,' said Kara. 'At least we know we won't have to look far if it does burn down again.'

'You could easily find out his name,' Ed said, getting Max under control again.

Kara looked at him. 'Rolf Ireland, aged sixty, married with two grown-up sons. Works as an accountant for a firm in the city centre. Lived here for thirty years; drives a Volvo SUV. His wife drives a Ford Fiesta.' She looked at the two men. 'He moaned at me before. I already knew his name; I just wanted to see if he would introduce himself this time.'

'He knew your name,' Bracken said. 'Just be careful.'

'It's a matter of public record since I own this property.'

'True. It's creepy how he would go out of his way to look you up,' Ed said.

'I know.'

'Maybe *he* needs a bit of Viagra in his life,' Ed said.

The other two laughed.

'You know Viagra was invented by accident?' Ed continued. 'They were trying to make something else, and they made the Viagra, and when they saw what it did, bingo. Happy accident.'

'Full of useless trivia, aren't you?' Bracken said.

'But I would advise you not to come here by yourself again, Kara,' Ed said, ignoring his son's remark. 'Max and Sean and I will come with you. And before you say anything, I know you can handle yourself, but it's a good idea to have witnesses, that's all.'

She smiled at the old man. 'Thanks, Ed. You're right. If I want to come here, I'll let you know. It won't be for much longer. A few weeks at most.'

'We'll come up any time.'

'Thank you, Sean.' She put a hand on his arm. 'I mean it.'

'I know.'

'Thanks, Ed.'

'Any time. You going back down the road?'

'Yes. Bit of TV for me. How about you two?'

'I'll drop Ed and Max off,' said Bracken, 'then I'll go and have a coffee with Chaz before she goes in for her night shift.'

'Did she say anything more about the note?' Kara asked.

'No. I told her to be careful.'

'I'll arrange for a patrol car to go by the mortuary regularly through the night,' Kara said.

'Thank you. She'll appreciate that.'

Both Kara's white BMW and Bracken's Ford

Mondeo were parked over to the side outside the garage, where a murder victim had once been found.

Kara got into her car and reversed, then drove out through the open driveway.

'You know I would put that bastard down if he had Max put down, don't you?' Ed said, but Bracken wasn't listening.

He was thinking about Viagra.

SEVENTEEN

'Viagra?' Chaz said. 'Of course I've heard of it. I thought you said you were only forty-five? Now you're trying to tell me you're seventy-five?'

'I would look good if I was seventy-five. But when I asked if you'd heard of Viagra, I didn't mean I wanted to use it.'

'Thank goodness for that. However, I have to say, I really do have a headache. Sorry.' She made a face at him before smiling.

'I can actually come round here without wanting to rip your clothes off.'

'If you'd been here half an hour ago, you would have seen me with my pyjamas on.'

'You had a lie-in?'

'I did. I couldn't sleep for a while. I tossed and turned, read some pages of a book, watched some TV. Had another can of lager, then finally crashed out with my fan set to freeze the balls off an Eskimo. I wish I had air conditioning like the Americans have.'

'Ed says his air conditioning is having Max wag his tail in his face. But God knows how he can stand it, having his dog lie next to him in bed. I mean, it's a double, but still. The room is small, but he doesn't mind. It's a roof over his head.'

'Oh, the poor guy. He works hard in that guest house.'

'Bob and Mary didn't ask him to; he just didn't want them to think he was a moocher.'

'He washes the windows, cuts the grass, cleans. He's a marvel,' Chaz said.

'As opposed to me, who's a lazy sod who doesn't lift a finger?' He raised his eyebrows at her.

'You're a paying guest in a guest house. Your dad wants to feel valued.'

'I know. He's trying to save his pension so he can add it to the insurance money to buy himself a new home.'

They sat down on the couch with a coffee. Chaz

still had a couple of hours before she had to leave for her night shift starting at ten o'clock.

'I got this in the mail today,' she said, reaching for a magazine on the coffee table in front of the couch. She lifted it and took the card out and handed it to him.

He took the card out of the envelope and read it, once, twice, before putting it back in the envelope and tossing it down on the table.

'You noticed it didn't have a stamp? It must have been hand-delivered.'

'Jesus, I didn't even notice that. That's even worse. They know where I live.'

'Enough's enough,' he said. 'Maybe you should come and move into the guest house for a while. Until we get this sorted. There are spare rooms available.'

'I don't think I want to be chased out of my own home, Sean. There have been some shitty things happening to me recently. I'm not going to run anymore.'

'Whoever it is knows your address, obviously. Just keep your wits about you when you're out and about.'

'I will, don't worry. But you'd better scoot. I have to shower then get ready.'

'Call me at any hour of the night if you need me,' he said and gave her a hug.

Then he left.

He had work to do.

EIGHTEEN

'It's still not too late to change your mind,' Bracken said to his ex-DI from Fife, Cameron Robb.

'What? Give over, boss. Sometimes we just have to do a little poking around, and I was only too happy to help.'

They were sitting in Robb's car. He had picked up Bracken from the guest house and now they were out and about. They had stopped at Balgreen Road, just round from the zoo.

Bracken had offered to drive Chaz to work, but she had refused. If somebody was watching her, she reasoned, he would see that as a sign of weakness. She thanked him and took her own car, promising to keep in touch before he went to bed.

Bracken had been holding the buff-coloured

folder Robb had brought with him, and now the car was stopped, he opened it and looked at the sheets of paper that had been printed out.

'Are you sure about this, son?'

'Checked and double-checked. I had one of my DS's go through it. Don't worry, I trust her like you trust me, boss. This is all correct.'

Bracken looked at the report again. Howard Wilson's mother was still alive when he died. He pre-deceased his father. He had one sister, not married, and she'd died in a car crash two years previously. Then his mother had died shortly afterwards.

'No immediate family,' Bracken said, looking over the paperwork again. He was starting to get hot in the car, so he turned the vent more towards him. 'A couple of uncles and a few cousins.'

'I ran them through the system. None of them have a record, and none of them live close by, according to the DVLA.'

'The card was hand-delivered. Somebody knows where she lives.'

'Bastard. You mentioned this other joker, Jim Brown. Maybe a couple of the lads and I should go and give him a wee talking-to.'

'As much as I'd like that, Cam, I don't want to

scare him off just now. He might back down, then go at her with a vengeance. Then *I'd* be the one talking to the bastard.'

'Just say the word. We could go back to the deserted farmhouse again.'

'Let's just go and see where he lives first, son. Before we set the dogs on him.'

NINETEEN

Chaz turned the key in the lock on the personnel door next to the roller garage door and turned to look around her before pushing the door open. There were plenty of cars going about and it was almost fully dark now. She stepped in quickly and slapped a couple of lights on. They would stay on all night, even if she had to go out with the van.

She put a hand in her trouser pocket and felt the pen there. It was a steel-body pen, hard enough to be rammed into an eyeball. The justice system in this country, this city, was well fucked. People walked out of court without getting a custodial sentence. A slap on the wrist. Well, she would ram a pen so hard into the bastard's eye, he wouldn't have to worry about appearing in court. It was called killing in self-defence.

She had had her doubts about Jim Brown right from the beginning, but had softened to him as time went on. Now, though, she thought he was a creepy bastard.

She walked in to Pamela Green's office, switching the kettle on. A nice cup of tea would calm her down. She could get her feet up and get her magazine out and read for a while.

Kettle boiled and tea made, she settled down by the phone, waiting for it to ring. She put her own phone down on the desk, along with her car keys. God forbid she have the keys in her pocket and inadvertently press the unlock button on her car.

She drank the tea, hoping the caffeine would kick in and keep her going, but no, she started yawning and then found she couldn't stay awake. She fought the tiredness, but the yawning became more frequent. Her eyes felt raw and she put her magazine aside. Maybe putting her head on the desk for a few moments would help. Maybe just a little power nap. Two minutes...

...became three hours.

Something woke her up.

A noise from upstairs. Faint. But there nonetheless. Maybe it was the fans kicking in, sucking the putrid air out of the soup kitchen, as they called the decomposition area.

Another noise. She sat rigid in her chair, holding her breath. This was a metal bowl after it had been dropped on the floor, the sound reverberating around the room.

The postmortem suite.

Her heart was racing. Suddenly, the pen in her pocket seemed totally inadequate, like taking a water pistol to a house fire. She sat and listened, hearing every creak in the building.

Then she noticed something.

The lights in the receiving bay were out.

They didn't go out by themselves. They weren't on a timer. Somebody had to switch them off. Which meant somebody had to have come along here, seen her sleeping and switched the lights off.

Her heart started thumping. The only illumination in the whole of the mortuary was the little lamp on behind Pamela's desk. It cast eerie little shadows.

She started breathing quietly. Maybe she should call Bracken, just to let him know. But then he would come rushing out here. What if it was just a bowl that hadn't been put back properly and had been balancing perfectly until a phantom breeze had come along and spoiled its equilibrium?

She tried to walk, but then her head spun a little and she put a hand down onto the desk to steady herself. She looked down, her eyes searching the desktop for her phone, but she couldn't see it. Her eyes were a bit hazy and her head felt light.

Where the hell was it? Had she knocked it off the desk when she had fallen asleep? She looked at the clock that was on the wall above the row of windows in the office. She was seeing double. She squinted, which helped a bit.

Almost five past...one. One! How could it be one in the morning? She had only put her head down five minutes ago. She looked for her phone again. It was gone. Along with her car keys. What was going on?

Yet deep in her heart, she knew.

Jim Brown. That was what was going on. The bastard.

Then the light in the office suddenly went out.

Her breath caught in her throat. Back here, it was pitch black. She could feel fear grip her, but forced herself to take deep breaths – in, out, in, out. Then, as thoughts ran about in her brain, she remembered what Pamela Green had said to her one day: 'If we ever get a power cut, remember, top-left drawer in my desk.'

Chaz hadn't moved, so she let her hand slide down to the top drawer. The one that Pamela had described as her junk drawer. Like the one Chaz had in her kitchen at home, filled with all sorts of stuff that had no appropriate place in a kitchen.

Her fingers found the drawer pull and she gently pulled the drawer out. The torch was a metal one, small enough to fit in the drawer. A torch that took AA batteries. Her hand skirted over junk and the sharp points of a staple remover jabbed at her fingers. She pulled them back for a second, then rummaged about again. Over on the right, she felt the metal barrel and pulled it out. Chaz remembered Pamela waving it about, like it was a weapon, and she had put her thumb on the bottom of the torch, pushing the button.

Chaz pressed the button and light shot out of it. The first thing she did was aim the bright beam of light out into the hallway outside the office. Both ways, left and right. Nobody there.

To the left, there was a door with a window set in it. There was no light on the other side of the door, but she hadn't really been expecting any. It led up to the viewing area and the public entrance.

To her right was the receiving area. She walked along there, moving the light back and forward, left to right, her heart pounding, her palm sweaty as she held the metal torch. She felt unsteady on her feet and a little light-headed.

The beam of light bounced off the windscreen of the van. She walked across to the door, turning round every foot or so, flashing the torch around. The personnel door was locked. Further along, there was a fire exit with a bar on the door. She walked along to it and pushed the door, but nothing happened. Again, the metal clanged, but still the door wouldn't open. It had to be wedged from the outside somehow.

The clicker for the garage door should be in the van. Thank God it was unlocked. She got in behind the wheel and looked around, but it was nowhere to be seen.

Somebody didn't want her to leave.

She got out, still shining the torch around, and headed through to the refrigeration room. There was a gentle hum in here from the automatic generator that powered the fridges. That and the fan that took out the smell from the decomposition room.

She went through the rubber doors, the top half opaque, and gently let the one flap close against the other. The stairs leading to the upper floor were here. She slowly walked up, turning at the small landing, making her way up to the door at the top.

Chaz was sure the main fuse box was up here. Somewhere near the PM suite. Maybe in a cupboard in the corridor, if she remembered correctly.

What if it isn't? The thought terrified her. There was another staff door that led out into the little street at the back of the building, High School Yards, but that too would be locked. She would have to smash her way through the glass, but she didn't think she would be able to do that.

The door appeared in front of her and she tried the handle. It opened, the hinges creaking slightly.

She felt the room spin again. She felt like she would slur her words if she started speaking. What the hell was wrong with her? The torchlight shone around the floor. She couldn't think straight. Where were the main fuses again? Did she even know in the first place?

She walked along the hallway, the light bouncing off the white walls.

Past the PM suite. Her heart was hammering. This was where she thought the noise had come from.

She thought she was going to die from fright.

Working in the mortuary, even at night on her own, hadn't bothered her. After all, there was nothing to fear from somebody who was already dead, was there?

Maybe the fuse box was near the small canteen they had. She turned the corner into the smaller hallway.

Then she heard the noise again. She wasn't even sure what it was, but this time it wasn't anything metallic.

It was a whisper.

She swung the light round and moved to the corner.

Her torchlight caught two black, faceless figures.

Then darkness took her.

TWENTY

Bracken got a text from Chaz saying that she was in the mortuary now and everything was okay. He nodded and put his phone away after replying to her.

'You can keep me right from here, boss,' Robb said. Bracken had told him he didn't have to keep calling him boss, since he didn't work for Bracken any more, but old habits and all that.

They were on Lothian Road now. Bracken directed him towards Bread Street and the Cowgate, and he looked over at the mortuary. There was probably a quicker way to Leith Walk, but nowadays streets were changing almost on a daily basis and that was the reason he gave himself as to why they were coming this way.

Truth was, Bracken wanted to be near Chaz in

case anything happened, but he felt comfortable knowing she was in the locked building.

'That's our mortuary,' he said to Robb as they passed by. The grey building looked even less friendly in the dark. Maybe if he hadn't been with Robb tonight, he would have gone in to have a cuppa with her.

They took St Mary's Street, and Bracken guided Robb down the Canongate and down Easter Road. It was a circuitous route, but it was easier than guiding Robb all over the place.

He took him along Dalmeny Street, past the old Scots Guards army hall, and they turned left into Leith Walk.

'Pull over here, son,' Bracken said, and Robb parked at the side of the road outside a Greggs bakers. 'He lives over there, in one of those flats above the shops. The stair door is next to that mortgage place.'

'You think we should go up and have a word with him?'

'Aye, let's go. If I speak with him and he gives Chaz some hassle, then you and the boys can come back and put the fear of death in him.'

'I'm sure they would love that,' Robb said as they got out of the car. 'It's been a while.'

'Aye, well, sometimes we have to look after our own, Cameron son. The courts are useless bastards. And don't get me started on politicians.'

Bracken and Robb had just got out of the car when Jim Brown came out of the stairway. He hailed a taxi and jumped in. They got back in their car, and before Robb could turn, the taxi was away, turning into a side street.

'Bastard,' Bracken said. 'I think I'll have to wait on him finishing work one day, then have a word. It's his lucky fucking night. Or unlucky, if he bothers Chaz.'

'He's a cocky wee bastard, right enough. Messing with her when he knows you're her boyfriend,' Robb agreed.

'May as well go home, pal. I'll text her, make sure she's alright.'

Bracken took his phone out and sent her: *If you need me, just call. Love you.*

It took a couple of minutes, but she replied: *Love you too.*

Except it wasn't her replying.

TWENTY-ONE

'Will you stop arsing about with that phone?' the taller of the two said.

'I'm just sending a text. This is her phone. He'll wonder why she didn't reply if I don't send one back,' the second one said.

The taller one looked round at the screen. *Love you*. 'Bloody soppy nonsense.'

'You don't have a loved one waiting at home, do you? You wouldn't understand.'

'I don't need to be tied down.'

'Bollocks.' He typed and sent it back.

'Are you sure she'll stay asleep?' Tall asked.

'Of course. I put in extra.'

Tall looked at him. 'You did what?'

'I put extra in the kettle. Make sure she stays

asleep. We could do Morris dancing in here and she wouldn't wake up.'

There was only one light on in the room, throwing shadows into the corners. Tall looked at him. 'It's not dangerous, is it?'

'No. It will just make her feel tired when she wakes up, but nothing a cup of coffee won't fix.'

'Right, let's get on with this.' Tall moved to one of the fridge drawers and pulled it open. Inside, an old woman's corpse lay under a sheet. 'Hello, Mrs Finnigan. I see the hair on your chin-chin-chinigan.'

'Fuck's sake. We're not entertainers at an old folks' home. Or do you want me to give you some time alone with her?'

Tall laughed until he started choking. 'Jesus, don't make me laugh, for God's sake. I don't want to collapse while I'm in here.'

'I'll shove you in one of those fucking fridges if you do, just so you know.'

'Good to see that you care,' Tall said.

'Yeah, don't get your fucking hopes up. All I care about is the product.'

'Clearly.'

'Just get a move on. I don't want to be in here any longer than necessary.'

Tall grinned and opened the zip on his holdall, and they both got to work.

TWENTY-TWO

'You're in late,' Ed Bracken said to his son.

'Jesus Christ,' Bracken said, stopping at the doorway of the residents' lounge. 'Creeping about in the bloody dark.'

'First of all, I'm sitting here, not creeping about. Second, I'm enjoying a bit of quiet with my Kindle.' A lamp with a remote control bulb was sitting on the end table, barely lit. Just like Ed wanted it. *Reading ambience*, he called it.

'I thought you only read comics?' Bracken came in and petted Max as the dog came over to him, before lying back down again.

'You're the only bloody comic round here. Where have you been anyway?'

Bracken sat down on the couch. 'You sound the same as when I was seventeen.'

'That's because you were going out on the lash back then. I was only looking out for you.'

'I was a big laddie, even back then.'

'Pain in the arse, you mean.' Ed bookmarked his page and closed the cover on the electronic reader. 'You look like you put your last pound in the johnny machine and it jammed.'

'For God's sake. You're an old man, you're not supposed to be thinking like that.'

'Well, are you going to tell me what's on your mind, or are you going to stare into space?'

Bracken blew out a breath. 'I was thinking about this thing with Chaz.'

'Some nutter writing to her? If you ask me, somebody's just trying to wind her up.'

'I know that, but who? And why? She seems to think it's because they pranked the new guy, but I'm having my doubts.'

'Oh, aye. Why? You and Cameron out and about, looking to push somebody's teeth in?'

'How did you know I was out with Cameron?'

'I know he didn't exactly pull up in the Batmobile, but I did see you get into a car and he was behind the wheel. That was a dead giveaway for a start.'

'See? This is why I'm the smartarse I am today. I take after my old man.'

'Just a pity you didn't get my charm and wit.'

'Aye, can you just imagine how far I'd have gone in life if I was a mini version of you?'

'That's it. The smart-arse-ness kicked in automatically. How you're not the chief constable by now is anybody's guess. But before I fall asleep from boredom, enlighten me as to where you were and who you gave a hammering to.'

'We did not hammer anybody. We're not the bloody Gestapo. We just looked somebody up.'

'Oh, I see. That Brown laddie. What's his name? Jim. He's already been found guilty in the court of Bracken.'

'I'm not saying that; I just had Cameron run the name through the system.'

'And? Is he an axe murderer?'

'Not that we know of. He has a flat on Leith Walk, he got a degree in biology and he's been working in the mortuary for a few months now.'

'Doesn't mean to say he isn't some kind of closet deviant.'

'That's what I'm worried about. What if he slipped under the radar?'

'If you know what university he went to, give them a call. See if he was some kind of headcase. Some people can be nice on the outside, but they have a dark streak. I should know, living with you.'

'You're too funny.'

'That reminds me, what did the report say?' Ed asked.

'What report?'

'The one you had done on Catherine's new boyfriend, Leon.'

'I hope you're not suggesting for one minute that I would go behind my ex-wife's back and have her new boyfriend checked out.'

'Of course I am. You were foaming at the mouth when we went round there last night. You were hoping that he had just been released from prison and you could throw him into the Water of Leith. But he's sound, isn't he?'

Bracken was silent for a moment. 'What are you reading anyway?'

'Just answer the bloody question: is Leon an upstanding member of society?'

'I hate you sometimes. You're going into a bloody home.'

Ed grinned. 'Fancy that; Leon isn't a chainsaw killer.'

'You're enjoying this, aren't you?'

'I am, actually.' Ed shook his head. 'To be honest, I feel relieved. As you said, Leon will be around Sarah, and I wouldn't want some scally bastard near her, not after what happened with her ex-boyfriend.'

'Hopefully, Leon will be good for Catherine.'

'Like Chaz is good for you.'

'We do okay.'

'You'd better look after her, son. I can see her being my next daughter-in-law.'

'Give over, will you? We're just going out, nothing more.'

'Did you call her earlier, to make sure she was okay?'

'I did, but she didn't answer.'

'Call her again,' Ed said, putting his Kindle tablet on the table next to the chair.

'It's late. It's gone midnight.' Bracken looked at his watch.

'It was gone midnight an hour ago, you wee bugger. I hope you and Cameron weren't on the lash, then having him drive home.'

'We were sitting in an all-night café down by the docks, chewing the fat.'

'You take advantage of that laddie, Sean.'

'Shite. He helps me out and he knows I always have his back if he needs me for anything.'

'You'd better make sure you honour that. Meantime, call Chaz for God's sake. If she's out on a call, she'll see you've called her and she'll get back to you.'

'Alright, don't get your string vest in a riot.'

They both turned as they heard somebody come into the lounge. Max looked up briefly, saw his jaws didn't need to spring into action and laid his head down again.

'Is everything okay?' Bob Long asked.

'Aye, it's fine,' Bracken said. 'Sorry if we woke you, but Ed forgot where the volume button to his mouth was.'

'Shut your hole.' Ed looked at Bob. 'Sorry if we disturbed you, fella, but I was reading until my son came in and disturbed the peace. Now he's hesitating about calling Chaz.'

'Why? What's wrong with her? Isn't she working tonight?'

'Aye, she is,' Bracken replied.

'He called her earlier but got no reply,' Ed told Bob.

'She's probably busy, Dad. There's only one staff member on through the night.'

'Aye, you'd better call her, Sean,' Bob said. 'Now you've got me worried.'

'Is everything okay?' Mary said, coming into the lounge behind Bob. She was pulling her dressing gown around her.

'I told you it would be Sean,' Bob told his wife. 'Nothing to worry about. Get back to bed before the whole bloody house gets woken up.'

'And they say romance is dead,' she said, smiling at Bracken. 'Love's sweet dream, right enough.' She left the room again, and Bob and Ed stared at Bracken.

'Are you both going to watch me while I call her?'

'Aye, we are,' Ed said. 'Hurry up now.'

'Nursing home, that's all I'm saying,' Bracken said to Ed before searching for Chaz on his contact list. He found the number and called her, but it rang until it went to voicemail.

'No answer,' he said.

'You need to go over there,' Ed said. Max sensed there was something amiss and stood up. 'Now he needs to pee.' Ed got up and put the dog's lead on and took him outside to water the flowers.

'Why don't you call control?' Bob suggested. 'See if the mortuary has had a call-out.'

'I was just about to do that.'

'Bloody liar. Go on, man, for fuck's sake. I'm like a nervous dad whose daughter has gone to the school leavers' dance and who thinks she's going to be deflowered.'

'Deflowered? You mean, she'll give him her orchid?'

'I'll give you bloody orchids in a minute. Make the call before one of us dies.'

Bracken knew he had been putting it off, because Chaz was a strong woman and he didn't want her to think that he thought she couldn't look after herself.

He made the call, and a few minutes later had his answer.

Ed came back in, and the German shepherd was revitalised now, looking around for his ball.

'The ball's away to bed,' Ed told him, but the dog was naturally suspicious and had fallen for that one before. He barked.

'Hush now, ya brat.' Then Ed looked at Bracken's face. 'I'm not even going to ask. Come on, Bob, get your car keys, son.'

'Right. Two minutes.'

'Whoa, whoa, where are you two going?' Bracken asked, standing up.

'The mortuary. Where did you think we're going?' Ed said.

'That'll be right.'

'Aye, son, that *will* be right. Bob and I are private citizens. We don't need the permission of the polis to go out in the early hours of the morning.'

'I can't let you do that,' Bracken said, holding up a hand.

'Listen, Sean, you know I love you, and Max loves you too, but he loves me more than he loves you, and if you should decide to physically restrain me, he will make sure you talk in a squeaky voice for the rest of your life. More than you do now.'

Bracken looked at Ed, then at Max, who was staring at him, his tongue lolling out of his mouth, looking calm. For now. Then he looked at Bob, who just nodded.

'Pair of bastards. I'll drive.'

'I'm bringing Max.'

'As long as you understand that a dog can't go into the mortuary.'

Ed smiled at Bob and they both shared a little chuckle.

'You're too funny, Sean,' Bob said.

'Oh God. I don't know why I fucking bother

with you two.' Bracken looked at his father. 'Keep the dog under control on the back seat.'

'Aye aye, Captain.'

'I'll just tell Mary we're off out,' Bob said, relinquishing the position of the head of the household in one fell swoop.

'We'll meet you in the car,' Bracken said. 'Do you need a mug of Horlicks before you go?' he said to his dad.

'Shut up. Get the bloody car open.'

They left the guest house, got into the Mondeo and waited for Bob, who seemed to be taking an inordinate amount of time saying goodbye to his wife.

'I hope he's not getting his leg over,' Ed remarked as he and the dog looked out the rear passenger window.

'For God's sake. We're not all demented perverts like you. Some of us think with our big brain.'

Ed laughed. 'Yeah, right. Chaz with black lingerie on and you'd be foaming at the mouth.'

'This is all getting documented for the director of the nursing home when he asks me why I think you need to be put into care.'

'Listen, son, if I ever get to the stage where I need my arse wiped and to be spoon-fed, I give you permission to put a plastic bag over my face.'

'Like the one you use when you go out on a date?'

'Haha.'

'Listen, the doctor won't have to toss a coin when he's asking me if I want to pull the plug or not.'

'Morbid wee sod.'

They saw Bob come out, zipping up his trousers.

'See? I told you he was getting his end away. Good to see it didn't take him long.'

'Like you in the old days: twice round the dance-floor and outside for a bit of how's your father.'

'Have a word with yourself.'

Bob got in the front passenger seat. 'I had a pish and my bloody zip jammed,' he said.

'No wonder you're out of breath,' Ed said. 'You must have been giving it laldy, trying to get it back up again. The zip.'

'Just ignore him,' Bracken said as they pulled out of the guest house car park.

The early hours of the morning meant the traffic was light, so Bracken put his foot down, heading down Balgreen, following the route Cameron Robb had taken earlier that night. He had the blue flashers going on the front of his car, although if he got pulled over, he didn't know what he would say to a uniformed patrol about the old codger in the back with a vicious dog. It was times like these that Bracken wished he had joined the fire brigade.

Down through the Grassmarket.

'I've had many a good night out down here,' Ed said, looking out the window at the pubs. 'Friday night, out with the boys. Good times.'

They drove under George IV Bridge and South Bridge before pulling into the mortuary car park. Bracken took his phone out and looked at the men in turn.

'If she answers, then she doesn't need to know we came here, treating her like a wee lassie. Agreed?'

The other men agreed and Max barked.

'One of you two needs his teeth brushed, and I hope for your sake it's the dog,' Bracken said to his dad.

Ed stuck up two fingers behind his son's back. Then Bracken hit Chaz's number on his phone.

It rang on the other end before going to voicemail.

He hung up and looked at the others. 'No answer.'

'Her car's there. The van might be inside, or she might be out in it,' Bob said.

'That's the choice, is it? The van's either in or out?' Bracken said.

'Don't take it out on me. We're all worried about Chaz,' Bob said.

'Aye, sorry. I just have that feeling in my guts.'

Ed opened the back door and Max hopped out.

'Where are you going?' Bracken asked Ed.

'I'm not going to sit on my arse waiting for you to ring that doorbell.'

The other men jumped out of the car.

Then Max started pulling on the lead.

TWENTY-THREE

Myra Taylor had never been one to call people her friend. Acquaintances, yes, but best friend? No.

Angela Monroe had been the closest thing Myra had had to a best friend. She was certainly somebody she trusted. *Had* trusted. Now she was gone. And whoever killed her was still walking about.

And Colin too. Two nicer people you couldn't meet. So she had thought until the other day.

Myra had her living room lights out and was staring out of the window to the darkness of the park where her friend had died. Myra thought she had been protecting Angela by getting her to run, but she had just pushed her into the arms of a killer.

She stopped her thoughts mid-flow.

Angela's possessions. Where were they? Nobody

had mentioned them, and nobody had asked about them. Her phone, her purse, but more importantly, her keys.

She thought back to last night, replaying the image in her head of after they left the pub. Hearing the sound of Beardy's feet behind them. He hadn't shouted a warning, which he wouldn't have done if he was trying to mug them. If he had been outraged at the way Myra had spoken to him in the pub, why hadn't he come after her? But when she had turned round, he had clearly been going after Angela. Who was the tallest out of the two of them?

He hadn't been angry; he had been going after his target.

He had reached out to Angela not to hit her but to snatch her handbag, the slim one she put on her shoulder, just big enough to hold her keys and purse.

The bastard had been trying to get her bag.

Myra drank more of her Bacardi and Coke and started pacing across the room. Her curtains were wide open, but there was no light to give anybody peering in some backdrop.

She was trying to think. The bastard had been watching them all night in the pub, which wasn't a coincidence. Myra had forced his hand, causing him to leave, and he had obviously been waiting outside, out of sight, to follow them.

Then he had made his move, not counting on Myra being able to take care of herself. Did he somehow manage to catch up with Angela? Shoot down another close and get to her before she could get into her apartment? Then answer the text that Myra had sent?

Then she heard it faintly. A light crash, coming from next door. Something falling, smashing. She put an ear to the wall, listening for any minute sound, but all she heard was her own breath coming out. There. A shoe stepping on a piece of glass, crunching it.

Controlling herself, she took the spare key for Angela's apartment and quietly opened her own front door and gently let the lock click behind her. The alcohol was messing with her brain.

She walked the few steps along the carpeted hallway and stopped at Angela's door. She put an ear to the door but heard nothing. She took the key out of her pocket, not thinking it through at all.

She slid the key into the lock and it glided in without making too much noise. Myra turned it and gently pushed the door. The hinges didn't squeak. The door opened quietly with no fuss.

She stepped into the hallway and put the light on. No time for covert action anymore. She moved into the square hallway and started moving faster and faster, pushing at doors, slapping at light switches.

As the lights came on, she saw there was nobody there.

Then she saw the broken mug shattered on the kitchen floor. Whoever had broken it must have left in a hurry.

She went into the bedroom and saw the bed sheets were messed up and the drawers had been opened, clothing tossed about the room. Then she went into the living room. The cushions on the couch had been slashed and the stuffing pulled out and thrown aside.

Somebody was looking for something.

Myra knew what it was.

And it wasn't in here. Not anymore.

One place she hadn't checked was the hall closet.

The one place the man had been hiding.

TWENTY-FOUR

It was cool now. Middle-of-the-night cool. Bracken had worn a lightweight jacket and had suggested to the others they grab something before they left, but oh no, the macho men had told him he was being a big fanny, that it was summer and it would be comfortable. He could see Bob was freezing his bollocks off.

'I'm freezing my bollocks off,' Bob confirmed. He banged on the roller door to the receiving area while Ed and Max checked the emergency door. Bracken checked the staff door, but everything was locked up.

'This place is tighter than...' Ed started to say, and the other two men turned to look at him, wondering where his mind was going.

'Than what?' Bracken said. 'If it's a member of a

religious community of women, I don't want to hear it.'

'I didn't even utter the word *nun*,' Ed complained. 'I was going to say, you.'

'Anyway, concentrate,' Bracken said, feeling tetchy now. He was eager to do something, to kick something, or maybe as a last resort, batter something with his extendable baton.

'What about the public door?' Bob suggested, as if reading Bracken's mind.

'I was just going to say that. You go with my dad round the back to check the upper-level staff door.'

'Come on, Ed, it's round the corner, up the hill in High School Yards.' Which was the name of a street.

Ed started rushing down the car park entrance into the Cowgate, Max, sensing something was up, starting to haul.

Out on the pavement, a drunk was walking towards them. 'Nice doggie!' he said, throwing a chip at the German Shepherd in the hope that it wouldn't clamp onto his bollocks. He stepped into the road as Max ignored the chip and snarled at the man.

If the drunk hadn't pissed himself by now, there was still the possibility of him checking his trousers in the morning and wondering at what point in his evening out he'd soiled himself. He excused himself with a quick, 'Fuck me, that thing's fucking mental,' lobbing another chip before doing his best to win gold at the Staggering All Over the Road event in the Pished-as-a-Fart Olympics.

Ed ignored him, but Max looked round more than once, not keen to turn his back on the human who may or may not be threatening his dad.

Ed and Bob turned into High School Wynd, which was a steep hill. 'If it was snowing, I reckon I'd be on my arse by now with the boy here pulling me up it.'

'We could build him a go-cart and he could pull us up hills. I don't know about you, but I'm fucked,' Bob said.

'Beats me why those daft bastards climb Mount Everest,' Ed observed. 'This is a short hill and already I'd like to set up base camp.'

'We need to go to the gym, Ed.'

They turned into High School Yards. There was a security fence round this area at the back of the mortuary, with built-in gates.

'Look, this one's open,' Bob said, pushing the gate with a foot. It opened lazily and Max started growling, the fur on his back going up.

'That's good enough for me,' Bob said, pulling an extendable baton out from an inside jacket pocket.

'You kept that when you retired?' Ed said.

'Fucking right I did. Don't tell his nibs. He'd only lecture me on how illegal it is, but I would rather be in front of a judge than in front of the man upstairs.'

'Too right. Me too. If some bastard comes at me, I carry a wee screwdriver. When I don't have this boy with me, that is.'

Ed approached the glass-paned door. It was ajar. Max started giving it the biscuit with the barking now.

'Better get in before he wakes up the whole damn neighbourhood,' Ed said, letting Max take the lead. As it were.

The dog pulled him along to the right as Bob took a torch out of his pocket and shone it along the corridor. There was nothing to see until they turned a corner.

Max started snarling until the torchlight picked out the still form of Chaz lying on the floor.

'Chaz!' shouted Ed. Then he turned to Bob. 'Go and get Sean!'

He let the dog go as he knelt down by Chaz's side, watching as Bob's light went round the corner with him. He quickly pulled out his phone and put the torch on, shining it on Chaz's face. He felt for a pulse and found one.

He heard voices, but Max wasn't barking now so he knew it would be Sean and Bob. Anybody else would have been hamburger meat.

'Christ! What happened?' Bracken shouted, kneeling down.

'We found her lying here,' Ed said, the big dog getting closer to him.

'Jesus. Is she...?'

'No. She's sleeping,' Ed said.

'Sleeping?' Bob said.

'Aye. Listen.'

They all held their breath. Heard the gentle snoring.

'Thank God for that,' Bracken said, gently shaking her. Then he looked at Bob. 'Why aren't the lights on?'

'Switches are not working. Somebody must have thrown the main breaker.'

'What the hell is going on here?' Ed said. 'No lights on. Chaz sleeping. Somebody's playing silly buggers. Come on, let's get her sitting up.'

Bracken and Bob got her into a sitting position, Bracken feeling her pulse. It was good and strong. 'Bob? Call for backup. There are some shenanigans going on. Tell them to get a few arses over here. Ambulance too.'

Bob turned away as Ed held on to Chaz. Bracken took his own phone out and put the torch on, cursing himself for not bringing a proper torch.

'Chaz? Chaz honey, can you hear me?' he said. She groaned a bit.

The big dog licked her face, and hearing her groan got him revved up, so as he licked her face harder. She lifted a hand to bat him away, but he kept on at it until Bracken gently stopped him.

'Max, lie down, boy.' The dog lay beside Chaz, guarding her.

Ed was bumbling about in the canteen, seeing if he could find the breaker panel. 'Where the hell would the panel be? Up here or downstairs, do you think?' he shouted through.

'I have no idea.' Bracken thought it was more worrying as to *why* somebody would want to switch it off.

Five minutes later, Bob showed some uniforms and the ambulance crew in.

Chaz was in a sitting position but still sleeping.

'Her name's Chaz Cullen,' said Bracken. 'She's my girlfriend. We just found her like this. She works here, but we couldn't get hold of her.'

'Is she on any medication?' the first paramedic asked.

Bracken looked stumped. 'I don't know.'

'You're her boyfriend and you don't know?'

'If she is, we haven't got to that stage of our relationship where we swap stories about what ailments we have and what the doctor's prescribed for them.'

They put her on oxygen and took her vitals.

'She was snoring like she was sleeping,' Ed said.

'Unconscious people can do that as well,' the paramedic said, looking at Ed like he had just scored an own goal in the Imbecile World Cup.

'Pardon me for offering an opinion,' Ed replied. 'I haven't had the benefit of watching *Blue Peter* on how to put a bandage on somebody.' He walked away with Max, uttering 'cheeky bastard' under his breath.

'Let's get her onto the gurney,' the man said to his partner, a young female who seemed to have a better disposition.

He turned to Bracken. 'I'm no doctor, but I watched the *Blue Peter* episode on how to tell if somebody's on something, and this lady has definitely been drugged.'

'Thanks, son. Forget the old man. He's no' right in the heid.'

'I heard that!' Ed shouted back.

Bracken helped get Chaz onto the gurney and

helped guide it to the door, then he stopped. 'I'll follow you to the Royal. I'll just be a minute.' Then Bracken turned to the four uniforms who were standing with Ed and Bob. The highest ranking was a sergeant, so Bracken addressed him.

'I'm DCI Bracken. This is Ed Bracken, my dad, with his dog, Max. This is ex-DI Bob Long. I'm going to leave them here with you. I want somebody to find that fucking breaker box and get the lights on in here. Somebody's been here arsing about, and they're going to regret it. I know Bob here is not with the force anymore, but he's forgotten more than you lot have learned. He's my eyes and ears. Get to it.'

He turned to Bob. 'I'll call you later.' He left.

Bob looked at the uniforms and the sergeant, who knew that most retired detectives still had friends on the force and one phone call would be all it took to fuck their career.

'Right,' the sergeant said, 'spread out and find that box. Then we'll report back to DI Long. Is that okay with you, sir?'

'That's fine, son. Let's get to it.'

'There's a metal bowl on the floor of the PM suite,' one uniform said after opening the door and looking in, then stepping into the large room.

'Maybe Chaz disturbed somebody,' Ed said,

keeping Max's lead wrapped round his hand. 'I hope to Christ they didn't touch her.'

They all had torches and started moving through the building.

Bob was walking down the corridor from the relatives' waiting room to the receiving bay when the lights came back on. He, Ed and Max rushed down and through the door.

'It was outside the refrigeration room,' a uniform said. 'There're generators that keep the fridges and the extractor fan going,' he explained. 'Somebody flicked the main switch to cut the electricity through the whole building.'

'Who the hell would switch the breaker off?' Bob said.

'Somebody who wanted to throw Chaz off her game,' Ed said.

'What's that down there on the floor?' Bob asked.

'It's a little blue pill,' the sergeant said. 'Do you reckon somebody here uses them?'

'I might be wrong there, son,' Ed said, 'but aren't they dead when they're in the fridges?'

'Aye, I think they're beyond pills at this stage,' Bob said.

The sergeant looked at a constable. 'Don't just bloody stand there – find a wee bag to put it in.

Professor Wall can see if it's something he dropped. Or one of the others.'

'It's called passing the buck,' Bob said. 'You'll be an expert at it after a few years. Isn't that right, Sergeant?'

'It is that, sir. It's a finely honed skill, passed down from the elders to the younger ones.'

The constable looked around him and was about to head towards the office when Bob pulled a Ziploc out of his trouser pocket.

'Old habits die hard,' he said to the younger man.

The uniform nodded his thanks and lifted the round pill by the edge with his fingernails, while the others looked on silently, like they were watching a game show and this contestant was on a hiding to nothing. But he got it in without it dropping back to the floor and rolling away out of sight.

'Right, we can leave it in Dr Green's office, and she can confer with Wall when he gets in. Leave it with a note, son,' Bob said, and the constable trotted away to the office.

'What do you reckon, sir?' the sergeant asked Bob.

'I wish I could say this is a bloody mystery, but Chaz got an anonymous letter from a man who died five years ago. Obviously somebody trying to put the shitters up her.'

'Mission accomplished, I reckon.'

'These doors were locked,' Bob said, nodding to the garage door and the other doors, 'but the top door was open. Like somebody had left in a hurry.'

'Maybe somebody was in here with Chaz,' Ed said. 'The paramedic said she looked like she had been drugged, but then where was she drugged? In that wee canteen upstairs, there are no cups out, no sign a cuppa was made. Doesn't mean anything until you see the remnants of a cup of tea in that office along the hallway.'

'Make sure the lab gets hold of that pill,' Bob said.

Then all hell broke loose.

TWENTY-FIVE

The doctor looked like he should be getting home now because he had school in the morning. A little bit of bum fluff was on his chin, and he had either overloaded on the hair gel or fallen head first into a chip pan.

'We've taken blood and sent it to our lab. She certainly is showing symptoms of having been administered some sort of sedative. Her vitals are great, and considering you told us that she doesn't take recreational drugs, isn't pregnant that you know of and doesn't drink alcohol on duty, I can only surmise she either took something by mistake or somebody slipped her something.'

'How could something like that be administered?'

'It's not a date rape drug, I can tell you that much, but it was probably administered in the same way: through liquid.'

'Has she woken up at all?'

'Not a hundred per cent. Normally, people wake up, even if they're feeling drowsy. But with all her vitals being good, I just gave her a little something to counteract whatever was given to her. Nothing that will interfere with her breathing and it's just a mild dose, but it will help her feel better when she does come round.' He looked at his watch: four a.m. 'In about three hours. You want to stay?'

'I would like to, but we have an important investigation on the go. I have to get back to the mortuary.'

'We have your number, so we'll keep in touch. I'll have somebody call you when she comes round.'

'Thank you.'

Bracken walked out of the Royal Infirmary into a chill air. Sunrise was a half hour or so away, but already the sky was beginning to yawn and stretch. He walked out of the white building, across to the car park where his Mondeo was. His insides were ablaze. Chaz had been through a lot since he had met her over six months ago, and now instead of living a peaceful life, here was somebody else causing havoc. Well, no more. He was going to encourage her to take the new job in the medical lab. No more night shifts. And if she was on-call and had to go into the hospital, she wouldn't be there by herself.

He got in his car, switched the blue flashers on and headed down Old Dalkeith Road. This would take him to the mortuary.

Where he hoped some answers lay.

But first, he had to make a phone call.

TWENTY-SIX

'What in the name of Christ is going on here?' Professor Simon Wall shouted. 'I mean, police all over the place. And where is that stupid woman who's supposed to be looking after this place?'

'That stupid woman is in the hospital, ignorant tosser,' Ed said.

Wall turned on him. 'And just who the fuck are you?' His eyes were blazing now and sweat was running down his face, which was turning a darker shade of red with each minute.

'You're worst fucking nightmare if you take another step closer to me,' Ed replied, barely keeping Max in check.

'Get that dog out of here! This is a mortuary, not

a dog park!' Wall screamed the last few words, spittle flying onto Ed's shirt.

Ed wiped the saliva away with his free hand. 'Manky bastard. Look at you. How are you sweating?'

'I'm telling you right fucking now –' Wall started to say, but Bob Long put a hand on his arm.

'Take it easy there, Prof.'

'Prof? What kind of respect is that? Nobody gives a crap these days! And you're not even on the force now! I'll have you fired!'

Bob looked at the sergeant, who just shrugged his shoulders behind Wall. They both picked up on the older man contradicting himself. Wall realised his mistake and turned to the sergeant.

'I'll have *you* fired for this!' he screamed.

'If anybody's going to decide that, it will be me.'

They all turned to the person who had just walked into the refrigeration room. Max wagged his tail at seeing Bracken.

'You need to lock him up, son,' Ed said as Max pulled towards Bracken. 'He's off his fucking heid.'

'I want to know just what the hell is going on in this place,' Bracken said, rubbing the big dog behind the ears.

'That's what I want to know! I come in here and find this place in a fucking shambles. Police everywhere; one of my staff not here when she should be on duty. It's a bloody disgrace, and let me tell you, heads will roll for this.'

'Somebody was in here tonight and tripped the switch in the electrical box,' Bracken said. 'We found Chaz upstairs unconscious.'

Wall looked at him for a second, and everybody who had gathered round for the cabaret was wondering if the professor would explode again. 'What? Unconscious? Is she alright? What happened? Did somebody attack her?'

No outburst this time.

'She's going to be fine. She just took a turn. So you see, Professor, we're all here because something happened to Chaz, not because we felt like getting up in the middle of the night to come down here for a rave.'

'Yes, yes, I'm sorry. I didn't mean to go off on one. I haven't been feeling myself lately.'

'Glad you got out of that habit,' Ed said in a low voice to Bob.

If Wall heard, he ignored it. Ed pulled the dog back to his side.

'Let's sit in Pamela's office and have a nice cup of tea,' Bracken said, leading the older man away along the hallway.

'That sounds just the ticket.'

Terry Jones appeared then. 'I'm sorry I couldn't get here any quicker,' he said. The head mortuary assistant was out of breath as if he had run here from wherever it was he had been.

'He's listed as a key-holder,' the sergeant explained to Bracken. 'I contacted control and they did the rest.'

'Good job. But let's get that kettle on,' Bracken said.

'Let me do that,' Jones said. 'I know where Pamela keeps her stash of Earl Grey.' He skipped round the professor, who didn't seem well at all.

He walked into the office and lifted the cordless kettle off its base and saw the cup with the remnants of tea in it and took both the kettle and cup out.

'Anybody else fancy a brew?' he asked, not meaning it, and he walked through to the refrigeration prep room, filled the kettle from the sink in there and poured the rest of Chaz's tea down the sink. He rinsed the mug and went back and stuck the kettle back on the base, pushing the button to start it.

'Right, let's get those Earl Grey bags in,' he said, fussing around like a mother hen.

'Will you calm down, for fuck's sake,' Wall said. 'You're making me dizzy.'

'Just trying to make sure you're taken care of, Professor.' Jones found the teabags and popped them in clean mugs that sat beside the kettle. 'Dr Green uses cream powder instead of milk,' he said.

'For God's sake, man, go away. You're like a fucking rash: annoying as all hell. Now beat it. We can fix our own tea.'

'Yes, sir. Just shout if you need me. I'll be out here.'

'Thank God he's leaving. This is his last week. I can't wait to see the back of him.'

Bracken made the tea, adding the powder to Wall's tea. The man blew on the surface of the tea before taking a sip.

'Apologies for snapping, Bracken. That man with the dog is your father, isn't he?'

'Yes, he is. We were worried about Chaz.'

'Apologise to him for me, will you? I seem so irritated just now. I'm snapping at the wife all the time. I don't think I've ever sworn so much in all my life. What the hell is happening to me?'

'I'm not sure, Professor, but we're going to get to the bottom of this.'

'I've not been sleeping at all. I think I need to go and see my GP. Maybe he can give me something to help me sleep.'

'Do that. Maybe you've been working too hard recently. It catches up with us.'

'I've not been working any harder than usual. Mind you, I'm not getting any younger.' Wall drank more tea. 'Please apologise to your father. I feel bad. We got off on the wrong foot.'

'Don't you worry about that. He's as tough as old boots,' Bracken said.

'Thank you.' More tea. 'You know, they asked me to come along here, but for the life of me, I can't remember why.'

'Because we came here and found Chaz unconscious.'

'Oh, yes.'

'Any idea who would want to shut down the power in here? Or why?' Bracken asked.

'Not got a clue, Sean. Chaz was the only one on duty tonight. I'll have that new lad, Brown, cover the shift. He can take today off and come in tonight instead.'

Bob walked along to the office and knocked. 'Apologies for getting you upset, Professor. Just to let you know Ed and I will be waiting outside. I know I'm retired –'

'Jesus Christ, I've known you for years. Get in here and shut the door.' Then Wall saw Ed waiting outside with the dog. 'Mr Bracken, join us.'

Ed stepped inside with Max.

'First of all, I apologise,' said Wall. 'I don't know what the hell is wrong with me. You, Bob, I've known for years. Have you ever known me to be like this?'

'I have to say, this is a first.'

'I know you must be under a lot of stress working in here, fella,' Ed said.

'Thank you. But usually I can handle the stress. In fact, I've been handling the stress for many years. I'm fifty-seven years old and feel like I'm seventy-seven. I just feel awful physically.'

Bob looked round to check nobody else was looking. 'I saw a blue pill on the floor in the refrigeration room, and we bagged it. Then, a little while ago, I saw another one. I bagged it and kept it to show DCI Bracken, just in case that first one went missing. Now, I'm not saying it would go walkies or anything, but there's some strange shite going on here.' He looked at Ed. 'Make sure nobody comes along that hallway, pal.'

Ed looked out of the window as Bracken and Wall looked up at the clear plastic bag.

'What the hell is that?' Bracken said.

Wall looked dumbfounded. 'I have no idea. It's not something we would use in here.'

'Somebody had it, and dropped a couple,' Bob said.

'I'll take it and have it analysed later today. The head of the lab owes me one. She'll do a quick job on it,' Bracken said. He looked at the other men. 'This doesn't leave this office, okay?'

They all agreed.

'Time to clear this lot out,' Bracken said.

'Agreed. They're giving me a bloody headache, Sean,' Wall said.

'I'll take care of it,' Bracken assured him, then he left the office and had a word with the sergeant.

'Do you still need me?' Terry Jones asked as he hovered around the refrigeration area.

'No, you can go. Professor Wall doesn't feel so good, but I'll make sure he gets home okay.'

'No problem. See you around.' Jones left, and the uniforms filed out, leaving the four men alone in the mortuary.

Bob came out of the office for a moment. 'Do you trust Wall?' he asked Bracken.

'I do, Bob. I've known the man for twenty years. You knew him as well. What is your gut saying?'

Bob blew his cheeks out. 'Somebody's up to something alright, but my gut says Wall isn't involved.'

'Me too. God knows what those blue pills are, but hopefully we'll get an answer from the lab later today.' Bracken yawned. 'Christ, I need a coffee.'

'Me too, but let's get Wall out of here.'

They walked back into the office, where Wall and Ed were having a conversation, Wall petting Max now.

'What a great start to a week's holiday, eh?' Wall said. 'I feel like shite and could sleep for a week I'm so tired, but I can't even sleep. No wonder I'm going mad.'

'Let me ask you something,' Bracken said. 'Do you have your own kettle in your office upstairs?'

'I do. God, being doctors we should know better than to drink all this caffeine, but we can't help it. Sometimes I'll have a brew late afternoon after a long day.'

'Last week, would you say you had been drinking out of the kettle every day?'

'Of course.'

'Who has access to your office?'

'Me, Pam and Terry. I generally don't keep it locked.'

'Do you ever get anybody else to make your coffee?' Bracken asked as Bob and Ed looked on.

'Terry makes it for me all the time.'

Bracken nodded. 'I think you should get home, Simon. You need to rest up. I can ask Pam to look in on you.'

'She's busy enough. I'll be fine.'

Bracken put a hand on his shoulder. 'I know your wife isn't a doctor, so I would feel better if a doctor looked in on you.'

'See how she feels about that then. If she wants to come round for a coffee, then that would be fine.'

Bracken's phone rang. He excused himself and went out into the receiving area to take it. He didn't recognise the number and he was ready to chew the arse off somebody who was trying to sell him an extended warranty for his car.

'Hello?'

Instead of an Indian voice, it was a Scottish female's. That was different.

'Inspector Bracken?' she said.

'Speaking.'

'It's Myra Taylor. I work in the lab beside

Angela. You told me to call you anytime, and I'm sorry about the late hour –'

'It's fine, Miss Taylor. Did you remember something?'

'Not exactly. You need to come here. To Angela's apartment. There's a dead man.'

TWENTY-SEVEN

Bracken was on the verge of handcuffing Ed to the inside of the car. 'Bloody hell. She said there's a dead man. You can't be waltzing in there with me. It sounds like a crime scene. She's meeting me in the underground garage. Just stay in the bloody car.'

Bracken had caught a uniformed patrol before they left and they had taken Professor Wall home.

Bracken stopped the car in front of the roller garage door that blocked the entrance to the car park. It opened silently and quickly and Myra Taylor was standing waiting for them. She waved them through.

Max growled, but Ed put his arm around the big dog. 'Hush your cakehole,' he said. 'You don't want to go scaring that lassie.'

'You not tired?' Bracken asked his dad.

'Tired? I'm bloody wired, more like. I haven't had this much fun in a long time.'

Bracken pulled into a parking space as Myra waited for them.

'You got that sample of the tea Chaz was drinking?' he asked from the driver's seat.

'It's in my pocket.' Ed reached in and brought it out, a little vial filled with tea.

'You filled it to the top. It isn't a piss sample, I hope – you forgot what you were doing and got carried away.'

'Shut your pie hole. I had a piss before we came down here, and none of it got near the vial, thank you very much.'

'Where was Max when you were using the facilities?'

'I was holding him,' Bob said. 'While you were sorting out a ride home for Wall.'

'Right,' Bracken said. 'Don't lose that vial, for God's sake. It's the only evidence we have and we didn't have a warrant.'

'Bollocks to a warrant,' Ed said. 'I know those overpaid twats would throw it out of court, but we wouldn't need a court to teach somebody a lesson. Eh, Bob?'

'That's right,' Bob answered.

'La-la-la,' Bracken said. 'I don't want to hear this bloody talk. You're not Charles Bronson.'

Bracken opened the door and Myra came straight across, if not at a gallop then at a fair trot. 'He's upstairs. Beardy. He's in Angela's apartment.'

'How do you know he's dead?'

'Because I killed him.' She looked at the car. 'Who are they? And is that a dog in there?'

No, that's my father, Bracken was going to say, but that would just start Ed off on a campaign of slagging each other off more than they already did, so he confirmed it was.

'Couple of friends of mine. We were out and about when I got the call. That's Max. German shepherd.'

Myra stepped closer and peered in through the windscreen. 'Does she bite?'

Ed or Max? 'He. And he doesn't bite me,' was all the assurance Bracken could give her.

'They can come up too. We could be in danger here. The guy who's on during the day, the concierge, is dodgy, and if he is, then maybe the others are too. The night guy looks like a weirdo. I'd break his neck if he came at me.'

Bracken was going to tell her that the other two men were going to stay in the car, but thought that having the big dog upstairs might cover his back. There was something about this woman that made him feel uneasy. He waved Ed and Bob out of the car, introducing them by their names, not his relationship to the older one.

'That's why I told you to come to the garage,' Myra explained. 'We can take the lift and bypass reception, where the night guy is at his desk. He won't do any rounds for security. He's concierge only.'

'Ed, Bob, this is Myra. She wants us all to go up to her apartment. There's been a situation in her neighbour's place. Don't touch anything.'

'Technically, we won't be at a crime scene if Myra has invited us up to her apartment,' Ed said.

'True.'

Max wagged his tail and sniffed Myra, giving her his seal of approval.

They got in the lift and took it to the third floor.

They stepped out of the lift into the carpeted corridor and walked along to Angela's apartment. Myra unlocked the door, but Bracken looked at the other two men and the dog. 'Go into Myra's apartment.'

'No,' Ed said. 'Our friend Myra has invited us up here, but we're waiting for her to answer the door.

We have every right to stand outside, waiting. We're not doing anything illegal, and it has no bearing on this case.'

'You sure you haven't been a lawyer in another life?' Bracken turned the door handle and he and Myra stepped inside. Max started to growl in the back of his throat.

Bracken looked at the dog. 'Time for this, I think,' he said, bringing out the extendable baton.

'Probable cause,' Bob was explaining to Ed. 'A police officer has the right to gain entry if he thinks a crime might have been committed.'

Bracken switched the hallway light on. 'Guide me,' he told Myra.

'Turn left into the living room. Her apartment is laid out differently from mine. He's in there.'

Bracken steeled himself and looked through the glass-paned French doors into the living room. He couldn't see much with the light being thrown from the hallway: a large TV on the wall opposite him and a couch over to the right. It was getting light outside but was still dark enough in here to cast shadows.

He opened one of the doors and walked in, going for the light switch on the wall, still facing the room. He flicked the switch and saw the room was empty.

There was a broken coffee table in the middle of the floor and a couple of cushions on the floor.

'You sure he was here?' Bracken said.

'Yes, of course. I should know, I was fighting with him. As you can see.'

'Let me check the rest of the apartment,' Bracken said, keeping his baton over his shoulder, ready to bring it down.

The kitchen was empty, as were the bathroom and the two bedrooms.

'There's nobody here,' Bracken said, coming back into the living room.

'Everything alright in there?' Bob asked, nudging the door open with one foot. Max saw that as an invitation to come in, but Ed held him back.

Bracken shook his head. His friend and his father at a potential crime scene. He couldn't have made this shit up.

'Apart from a broken table, there's really no evidence of a fight or somebody being killed in here.'

'I thought he was dead. I checked his pulse. There wasn't one.' She looked doubtful. 'Was I just dreaming this?'

'I think that stress does a lot to people's minds. Come on, let's get you back to your apartment. Get you a nice cup of tea.' Then Bracken stopped himself. Put the lights out and guided her out into the hallway.

'Before you go into your apartment, I want to ask you something: have you ever seen these before?'

She looked at the little blue pill sitting in the Ziploc bag. 'What's that?'

'I was hoping you could tell me. I just found it in Angela's bedroom. Another one. We already have one at our lab. What is it going to tell us?'

'Oh my God. She told me she didn't.'

'Didn't what?'

'Can I use the bathroom?' Ed asked. 'I need to pee.'

'You said you had a pee before you came here.'

'I did. I need one again. Once you uncork the bottle and all that.'

'Aye, I'd better have a pee an' all,' Bob said.

'You're like a couple of bloody old men,' Bracken said.

'We *are* old men,' Ed said.

'Speak for yourself there, chum,' Bob said.

'Once you got to fifty, it was all downhill,' Ed confirmed.

'Why don't we go into my flat? I don't want to talk out here,' Myra said.

They secured Angela's apartment and went into

Myra's, where Ed assumed it was okay to use the bathroom. He asked Myra in a low voice where it was.

'That door on the left,' she said, and Bob held the dog while Ed went in first.

'I hope you left it as fresh as you found it,' Bob said when Ed came out, handing the German shepherd back.

'Of course I did. I'm in somebody else's house.' Ed went into the living room as Bob cursed after shutting the bathroom door.

'I can show you me having the fight with Beardy,' Myra said, walking over to the kitchen area and putting the kettle on.

'A cuppa. Smashing,' Bob said, coming into the living room. 'I'm starting to flag a bit.' And to Ed: 'You should have lit a bloody candle in there.'

'I don't know what you're talking about there, chief.' Ed sat down with the dog at his feet. Bob sat on a chair, warning Ed that if Myra complained about the toilet being honking, he would drop the old man right in it.

'Just blame it on Max,' Ed said in a low voice. 'I do that all the time.'

'What? Keeking your bloody Ys or blaming Max? They have medication for that, by the way.'

'Try saying it a bit louder. I don't think they heard you over in the Palace.'

'What are you two whispering about?' Bracken said.

'Nothing,' Ed said quickly.

'Conspiring about something. I can tell you're guilty.'

'How?' Ed asked.

'Your lips are moving.' Bracken turned back to the kitchen, where Myra was pouring the coffee. Ed made a face behind his son's back.

'No decaf, I'm afraid,' Myra said. 'Milk and sugar?'

'Moo and two,' Bob said. 'Thanks.'

'Just moo for me,' Ed said. 'Maybe a wee Hobnob?'

'I only have Rich Tea,' Myra said. 'Sorry.'

'That's alright, love.' To Bob: 'Cardboard. That's the sort of biscuits they start dishing out on the lifeboat when they're done eating the other passengers.'

Myra came across with two mugs of coffee and put them on the coffee table in front of the couch. 'Do you want the TV on?'

'Aye, go on then,' Bob said. 'We can watch some sports.'

Myra fired the TV up with the remote and handed it to Bob.

'*Tom and Jerry?*' he asked Ed in a quiet voice as Myra went back over to Bracken.

'Aye, go on then, son.' Ed settled back on the couch and drank some of the coffee, hoping the woman hadn't spiked it. He didn't want to be blowing about the flat like he was demented. Bob picked up his mug and sipped at it.

Bracken sat at the high bistro table with barstools and waited for Myra to have a sip of her coffee first.

'Don't worry, I haven't spiked it.'

Both men on the couch put their mugs on the coffee table at the same time.

'Honestly. It's pure Maxwell House.'

Bracken drank his. 'Do you want to tell me what's been going on, Myra?'

'I will. I mean, I'm not involved in anything, but I can tell you what I know about Angela. That man would have killed me tonight if I hadn't got the better of him.'

Bracken looked sceptical.

'Listen,' Myra said, 'I can show you. See that clock up there?'

Bracken looked at the plain white clock and nodded.

'It has a hidden camera in it. Angela has the exact same one. We both got one, so if we brought a man home, we would text the other one, and they could keep an eye on things on the camera. Like, if it wasn't going well, we would either call or just ring the doorbell. If it was going well, then the camera only sees into the living room. I can show you footage of tonight.'

Myra played around on her phone and Bracken was glad he didn't have some such thing on his phone. It took him all day just to open the weather app. He looked quickly over to the TV, then did a double take. The two men were watching cartoons. He wondered if it was too late to deny knowing them.

Myra didn't notice, or at least was pretending not to notice, the episode of *Charlie and Lola*, and showed Bracken her phone. On it was a video, the picture a bit grainy but it got the job done. They watched Angela's living room from the wall clock's perspective. Myra coming into the living room, and then the man with the beard appearing and grabbing her round the throat from behind by wrapping an arm around her neck, putting her into a chokehold.

Myra turned her head, lifted one of the man's legs and pushed with all her weight. They fell backwards and the man had to let go to put his hands out to save himself. Myra rolled off him before he could grab her and was on her feet. Beardy was just as quick, jumping up, but now they were facing each other.

Beardy brought out a knife from a pocket in his jacket and thrust it towards Myra. His right arm took aim at her midriff, but she sidestepped it, grabbed the wrist with one hand, snaked her left hand round to connect with Beardy's jaw, then put a leg behind his and threw him backwards.

The knife flew out of his hand, but once again he recovered quickly and launched himself at Myra, putting his hands round her neck. Myra countered by bringing her right arm up and over Beardy's arms, twisting her body to the left, then rammed her right elbow into Beardy's face. He yelled and let go, and then Myra turned round and punched Beardy in the throat.

He went down, clutching his neck, writhing about in agony.

Myra ran out of Angela's apartment and out of sight of the camera.

'Wow, that must have scared the crap out of you,' Bracken said.

'To be honest, it did, but I felt more adrenaline than anything.'

'Where did you learn to fight like that?'

'My dad was in the Marines.'

'Do you know who this guy is?' Bracken said. He saw that Ed and Bob thought that an appropriate amount of time had passed after Bracken had taken a drink of coffee, and since he hadn't keeled over, they picked theirs up again.

'No, but I wasn't sure what to do, so I sat in here in the dark. I remembered the camera a while later. I should have called the police, but I thought I'd killed him. Now I know I did. Watch this.'

She played around with the videos in the cloud and brought up another one.

It showed a man coming into the room, dressed in black. He was wearing a baseball cap and was wheeling a gurney with a body bag on it.

'What the hell?' Bracken said.

'Now look and you'll see Beardy really is dead. That man didn't know Beardy was dead, so why would he come in with a gurney? I'll tell you why: I think he was coming for me. He was coming along to my apartment and saw Angela's front door was open. He ended up taking Beardy away. Beardy was sent to kill me, and

he was the one doing the cleaning up. I think Beardy
was sent to kill Angela the other night, but I got in his
way. I think he found her later, killed her and dumped
her in the park to make it look like an accident.'

'You think he killed Colin Paisley as well?'
Bracken shot a quick glance over to the couch,
thinking maybe he'd made a mistake earlier and only
thought he saw cartoons on, but no, there they were.

'I have no idea. I suspect he did.'

'Do you know why they were targets? Why you
were a target?'

'I think it was because what Angela and Colin
were up to. And Beardy found out that Angela tried
to get me involved, but I didn't want anything to do
with it.'

Bracken thought she was talking in riddles and
knew he had to coax it out of her.

'What were they up to?' he asked her gently.

'They were drug dealers.'

TWENTY-EIGHT

The sun was doing its warm-up exercises as it came over Arthur's Seat.

'Is that what those little blue pills are? Some narcotics?' Bracken asked Myra.

She nodded. 'They must be. I'm not sure. I haven't seen them before. I couldn't believe it. Myra and I were talking one night, and she just came out with, did I want in. I asked her...'

'...in what?'

Angela Monroe had never been shy and beating about the bush wasn't in her psyche.

'Do you want to make some serious money?'

They were sitting in the pub in the High Street, their usual haunt. 'I'm not wanting to be a stripper; I already told you.' Myra smiled at her friend.

'I'm serious. You know the work we've been doing. We get paid decent wages for doing all the bloody hard work. I just got to thinking, why don't we reap some of the rewards? We could use some of that stuff for ourselves. Not the end product, of course, but some of the lesser ones. The ones we had to reject because it wasn't good enough for them. Well, it could be good enough for us. You know, same result, just for a shorter time. We could make a fortune.'

'God, Angela, that sounds too risky. I don't want to go to prison.'

Angela laughed. 'You won't go to prison, because you won't get caught.'

'Famous last words.' Myra drank some of her Bacardi. 'Look, don't think I'm not grateful, but you do what's best for you. I would like to settle down one day, and I don't mean in a prison cell. Thanks anyway...'

Bracken looked over at the couch and saw two heads tilted sideways. Bob and Ed would both be snoring in a minute.

'What was this drug they were selling?'

'That blue pill you have? We were working on a classified drug for the US Air Force. They have their own labs, of course, but one drug they tried out ended up with a lawsuit. It was flawed, and the Senate was pissed off at them. Two airmen died. The Americans already have a Go pill. A pilot can fly a plane to Iran, bomb the shit out of it, then fly back, all while staying awake. Which is all fine and dandy, until they need to sleep. So they developed the Slo pill. This brings them down to earth, as it were.'

'Were you successful in developing a new pill for them?'

'Oh, yes. We made quite a few different types, but they weren't quite right. Then we got close with one in particular, but it didn't keep the pilots awake long enough, so it was tweaked to perfection. Same with the Slo pills. We made a new one with less side effects. But it was the rejects that Angela and Colin were wanting to sell. Obviously, they weren't going to need a pill that could keep somebody awake for four days or whatever, but this pill that was rejected, it could keep you awake all night. There were no downsides to them at all. They would make you feel good and give you energy, and when you needed to sleep, you'd pop a Slo pill, which will let you get by on two hours' sleep, making you feel like you had eight. Not good enough for the military, but good enough as a recreational drug.'

'Good God. And they were going to sell this?' Bracken said, hearing the first snore.

'Oh, yes. They had a buyer. But then Angela came to me one night and told me there was a problem with the drug. It had a side effect after all.'

'Which is?'

Myra drank more of her coffee even though it was getting cold. 'Aggression. The drug lasts longer in the system than anticipated, and if they don't take a Slo pill, the person gets more irritable and then outright aggressive. Angela knew this because they were slipping the pills into people's drinks to see how they would react.'

'Obviously people they knew.'

'Yes.'

'Were you one of them?'

'Me? No, I don't think so; I just know how to fight. But she said they had started to watch the results.'

'And Colin Paisley knew about this side effect, I assume?' Bracken said.

'Oh, yes. He wanted to stop it, but it was too far along. The batch had been made and the deal was going through. They all stood to make a fortune off it.'

'You think Angela and Colin wanted to stop and that's what got them killed?'

Myra put her mug down. 'I think so.'

'Why would they then turn their attention to you if you don't have anything to do with it?' But Bracken knew the answer: Myra knew too much. She wasn't supposed to be part of the plan, but somehow Angela had let slip that she had told Myra about the plan and now they wanted to kill her too.

'You said they were testing the drug on people. Is that how they found out about the side effects? Just watching them?'

'With the last batch. Angela told me they had a unique system of getting rid of the old batches that hadn't worked out. They couldn't flush them down the toilet, and they couldn't dispose of them in the same way that legit samples are destroyed, so they brought somebody on board who could help with that. Foolproof, Angela said. She didn't tell me who it was, but I think I know.'

Bracken looked at her.

'The man who took Beardy away. I think he was the one.'

TWENTY-NINE

There was only one thing to do at short notice that may save Myra's life: put her in a room at the guest house.

Four hours later, Bracken had had three hours' sleep and was woken by a car horn outside. He looked at his clock and saw it was just after nine. He hadn't meant to sleep this long.

He got up to use the bathroom and wondered what the Go pills were really like. He knew about people taking uppers to get them going and downers to bring them back to earth, but military-grade pills would be on a different level.

After a quick shower, he called the Royal to enquire about Chaz. Bob had insisted that he drive out to the hospital to pick her up, but the doctor said they wanted to keep her in during the day with a possibility of afternoon release. Bob had slunk off to bed, and Mary hadn't been quite sure that he hadn't been messing about with Myra until Ed convinced her.

Dressed, Bracken went downstairs to see about getting more coffee. The other guests had finished their breakfast. He missed old Mr and Mrs Clark, who had moved into a small retirement flat along the road.

Natalie Hogan, once a GP until a painkiller addiction had taken her career, was sitting in the lounge watching TV. Her young son, Rory, was playing with his cars on the coffee table.

'Be careful, you'll scratch the top,' she said to her boy. Natalie was Bob and Mary's niece, and she worked in Tesco in Corstorphine and helped out with chores around the guest house. Much like Ed.

'Good morning. You look like crap,' Natalie said with a smile.

'Same to you,' he replied. 'The good morning bit, I mean. And thank you. I've had a few hours' sleep.'

'That's not good, you know.'

Bracken sat down with a coffee. 'Tell me about it.'

'You want me to make you some breakfast? I was

helping out this morning. I have to go in for an afternoon shift.'

'You don't have to do that.'

'It's how I help out Mary. One of the little things I do. Couple of bacon rolls?'

'Go on then. Thank you.'

Bracken watched TV and rolled a couple of the cars around the table with Rory until Natalie came back.

'Thanks a lot,' he said, wolfing down a roll.

'Why were you out so late?' she asked him.

'Chaz collapsed at work.'

'God, is she okay?'

'She is, but we think she was drugged.'

'Drugged? Who would want to do that?'

'I wasn't sure, but now I'm getting an idea. Have you heard of Go pills and Slo pills?' he asked her.

'Yes, of course. The military use them. They can wreak havoc on your body.'

This was the part where Bracken thought about crossing the line, and normally he wouldn't, but he trusted Natalie. 'I need to run something by you, but in the strictest confidence. I don't need anybody else knowing about this. People have been dying because of it.'

'Not sure I like that part, but go ahead.'

Bracken tucked into the second roll. Swallowed before carrying on. 'Somebody has been making Go and Slo pills. They've made a...how would you say it...a domestic version. Not as potent as the pilot version, but they're selling them. Thing is, there's a side effect they didn't know about until now. Aggression.'

'That would be the drug playing about with the brain's receptors. The brain needs to sleep, but the chemicals have altered the running of the brain, and now it's thinking, *Oh, okay, I can sleep later*. But the Slo pill will make them come down or else they might be going for days. I've seen the effects on people who have been on something and sleep deprived.'

'I don't think Chaz was given a Go pill but a Slo pill. That would knock her out, wouldn't it?'

'Yes. They've probably created a very potent drug with dextromethorphan in it. That's what's in sleep medicines. If they made a strong one, it would really knock a person out, especially if it had been designed to counteract the Go pill. Like when you see the tractor unit of a truck driving along without the trailer to pull. Just the cab part itself. It can move a lot faster without the weight. There's nothing to counteract the weight of the trailer. That's the same with the Slo pill; they aren't supposed to be given without the Go pill being taken first. The drug in her system has nothing to fight, there's no resistance, and so it will knock her right out.'

'The doctor says she might be able to come home this afternoon.'

'I would be very surprised if that's the case, but it depends. This new drug that somebody has created might not have the same effect as the usual ones.'

Bracken finished his roll, and Natalie said she would take the plate away. He finished his coffee and left the room. A thought had struck him, and he needed to meet up with Jimmy Sullivan.

First, he had to have a talk with Myra Taylor.

THIRTY

'You sure about this, boss?' Sullivan said, driving towards the mortuary. He was spending more time here than at the station. Which wasn't too bad, so long as he could leave the place again.

'No, not at all.' Bracken had gone over the events of last night and had finished with an idea he had.

He called the lab and spoke to the head technician.

'The tea had traces of dextromethorphan in it. The vial you handed in was enough to get an accurate reading. There was enough dextromethorphan to make her sleep for hours. Nothing lethal, just enough to make her sleep like she had taken cold medicine.'

'Christ. Will it have a lasting effect on Chaz?'

'I'm not a doctor, but I don't think so. More like if she had drunk two of the little cups of cold medicine, the cups that come with the bottle. Not deadly.'

'Thanks, pal.'

'We're still working on that blue pill that was handed in.'

Bracken cut the call. Then he made a call to Simon Wall, and the man was livid when he heard what Bracken had to say.

'I'll meet you there,' he said, hanging up, and sure enough, Sullivan had just parked his car when Wall came booting into the mortuary car park. He slammed his car door after getting out.

'He looks worse than you, and that's saying something. I mean, you're no oil painting at the best of times, but –'

'Shut up, Jimmy, and don't mention how bad he looks. There's something wrong with him and he's been suffering from aggression. Trust me, I saw him in action earlier this morning and it's not pretty.'

'Morning again, Professor,' Bracken said.

Wall shook his head. 'This is so fu...messed-up. Are you sure you know this is happening?' His hair was short, so it wasn't sticking up, but his eyes were red and he looked like he had dressed in a hurry.

'Not definitively, but it's the best theory I have right now.'

'Fuck it, let's go inside. This is my mortuary and I'll be damned if I'll allow somebody to hijack it for their own purposes. Is Jim Brown inside?'

'I didn't want to call ahead and give them a heads-up.'

'Little bastard. I'll see he never works in the medical field again. He'd better learn the phrase, *Do you want fries with that?*, because that will be the highlight of his career when I'm finished with him.'

'Simon, we need to keep it cool for now. Or else this won't work.'

'Alright. I'll make the call and then hope he takes the bait.'

Wall took the lift up to his office.

Bracken and Sullivan walked along to Pamela's office, but she wasn't in.

'Good morning, detectives!' a voice said from behind them. Jim Brown approached and smiled at them.

Little bastard.

'I want a word with you,' Bracken said.

'I heard about Chaz. I'm sorry.'

'Sorry that you wrote that note and scared the crap out of her?'

'No, I meant I didn't mean to scare her last night.'

'Explain yourself, son.'

Brown shook his head. 'I was at my girlfriend's last night. Her parents are away on holiday, so she asked me to bring her here. She's a goth. She said she likes this sort of place. So, me being the arsehole, I brought her along to show off. I let myself in the top door and took her in to see the PM suite. She wanted to do it on a steel table, but I drew the line. First of all, that's not my thing. Then the bloody lights went out and I knocked a bowl onto the floor, where it clattered. We stayed in there because I knew Chaz was downstairs. I thought she might not have heard it, but then we saw the torchlight coming up the stairs. Chaz looked like she was drunk. My girlfriend and I had hoodies on, so we rushed past her and got out.'

'Why did you write the letters to her claiming to be Howard Wilson, the dead man?'

Brown shook his head. 'I swear, that wasn't me. I have no reason to do that to her.'

'And you didn't flick the breaker in the electrical box either?'

'No. I don't think it was Chaz either. When we got back in my car, I booted it down the hill and drove past the front of the building, and I saw a vehicle parked there, right up against the emergency door.'

He described it in detail.

'Stick around. We'll talk about this further.'

Brown nodded and walked away.

Wall came back down in the lift. 'I called him.'

'How did he sound?'

'Like he was going to shite himself.'

'He very well might when we talk to him. When's he coming?'

'He's coming right now, as we speak.'

THIRTY-ONE

'This is ridiculous,' Marcus King said, storming into the mortuary.

'It's on behalf of the family. They have that right, as you know,' Professor Wall said. He was calm about it, a far cry from hours earlier. 'If they want another postmortem done, they can have one.'

'Everything has been planned for her funeral. It's just inconvenient.'

'I'm sure the old woman dying was inconvenient for the family,' Bracken said.

'I have old Mr Rogan to take today as well. I take it that's acceptable?'

'He's waiting in the drawer next to the old woman,' Wall said. 'Help yourself. I'll be upstairs if you need me.'

They walked along the hallway to Pamela's office, then stepped inside, closing the door behind them.

Jim Brown walked into the refrigeration room and stopped. 'Oh, sorry, I didn't know you were in here.'

'Get out!' King shouted. 'This is a private moment with me and my client. You know that, don't you?'

'I'm sorry,' Brown said, stepping out of the large room. He walked along to Pamela's office, where Sullivan was looking out of one of the windows. Brown put his thumbs up then left, heading towards the stairs.

Bracken, Sullivan and Wall walked out and went along the hallway. Bracken went through the rubber door of the room. King spun round. He had taken the sheet off the old woman and it was obvious he'd had his hands inside the body cavity.

'Is this what you're looking for?' Bracken said, and the three men brought the bags of blue pills out from behind their backs.

'I don't know what you're talking about.'

'Come on, do you think we're daft? We know you put them in there, because we took them out half an hour ago.'

'I don't know what you mean. I'm just here to look at my client. Now that I have, I'll put her back. I don't know what those are.'

'Really?' Sullivan said. 'You had two funerals last week, and we're getting exhumation orders for them both. Will we find anything? Who knows? But your cohort, Angela Monroe, told her friend that a lot of batches were made that didn't quite make the cut. Are they in your other clients? I think they are. We'll exhume every one we need to. It was the foolproof way to get rid of the drugs, you said to Angela.'

They held the bags by their sides.

King tried to make a run for it, pushing past Wall, who was the path of least resistance. But then he ran into DS Tam Gale and DC Lennox Docherty, who were waiting outside.

'What's going on?' Jim Brown said, having reappeared with Terry Jones by his side.

'How should I fucking know?' Jones snarled at the younger man.

'Let me go, you bastards!' King said to the two detectives who were restraining him.

The lift doors opened and Pamela Green stepped out. 'What's going on here?' she asked Wall.

'I think you know fine well, Pamela,' Bracken said. 'After all, you were the mastermind behind this.

Joining forces with Angela Monroe so you could manipulate Marcus King, make him dance like a puppet to your tune. Well, no more. You're under arrest.'

'What are you talking about, Bracken? I did no such thing.'

Bracken turned her around and put the hand-cuffs on her.

'You're very clever, I have to admit. Creating this whole façade, being a pathologist, using this poor sap as your underling. What made you do it? Money?'

'I don't know what you're talking about.'

'We found the drugs in your tea that you had in your office. The tea that Chaz drank. We've had it analysed. You should be ashamed of yourself, getting Marcus King to do your dirty work. He's just the wee laddie following your lead. I feel sorry for him, you being the manipulative bitch you are.'

'Shut the fuck up!' Marcus King said. 'She has nothing to do with this! You think I'd take orders from a whiny bitch like that? Go fuck yourself. It was Terry and I who ran this end.'

'Shut up, you stupid bastard!' Jones said, then he turned to run, but Jim Brown stuck his foot out and tripped him.

'Oops,' Brown said as Gale hauled the man to his feet.

'You're under arrest,' Gale told him.

Bracken took the cuffs off Pamela. 'If this pathologist gig doesn't work out, there's a career on the stage for you.'

'I did do rather well, didn't I?' she said.

Marcus King was struggling as uniforms piled into the refrigeration room. 'You were fucking playing me, Bracken.'

'Yes, I was. I knew your ego couldn't stand the thought of me thinking you had a woman controlling you.'

'Bastard!' he screamed as he was hauled out with his partner in crime, Terry Jones. But before he left the building, Bracken stopped Jones.

'Was it you who put the note on Chaz's car? And put the card through her door?'

'I just wanted to scare her enough that she would call in sick. Just to give us a bit of freedom this week. We didn't think it through enough, obviously.'

'How did you know it was Jones?' Pamela asked Bracken once the man had been taken away.

'The way he scuttled about grabbing the kettle and Chaz's cup. He wanted to make sure there was no trace evidence of the drug, but Ed had already filled a vial with the tea after I called him. He left some in the cup so it wouldn't be obvious.'

'Do you think Marcus or Terry killed Angela and Colin?'

'Marcus had a man working for him. I think he did the killing, based on other evidence. King and Jones will be going away for accessory to murder, but the drugs charges will nail them.'

'What about the man who did the killing? Have you got him?'

'I think we'll find him at Marcus's premises when we search it. He was killed in self-defence after he attacked another woman. She has it on security video.'

Pamela shook her head. 'I'm still shaking, Sean. When you told me and asked me to help...I still can't believe Terry was involved.'

'Good job, Sean,' Wall said, coming across to them and patting Bracken on the shoulder.

'We got Jim Brown to help. Just so you know, he came here after dark and was showing his girlfriend around and that's when the lights were put out by King and Jones. He deserves a reprimand, but on the flip side, he did tell me he saw a hearse parked at the emergency exit, right against the door. That helped. And he agreed to help us today. I would go lightly on him. He's a good member of staff, but I told him if I found out he was creeping about here at night, I'd kick his arse.'

'I'll have a talk to him,' Wall said. 'I need him to do the night shift this week while Chaz recovers.'

'Good man.'

'That was a nice wrap-up, boss,' Sullivan said.

'Except it's not over,' Bracken said.

THIRTY-TWO

Myra Taylor had decided that she wouldn't be going back to the lab. As much as she'd loved working with Angela and Colin, they had brought so much grief into her life. Besides, the legitimate contract for the Air Force was fulfilled now, so she could find pastures new.

The knock was light, as if somebody outside her front door didn't want to disturb the residents inside. Which didn't make sense.

Myra walked to the front door and looked through the peephole before opening the door.

It was Wish-washy himself, William Potter. 'Oh my goodness, Myra. You're safe – thank God.'

'William, please come in.' She stepped aside to let her boss into the apartment.

'Thank you. I was worried when you called, saying you were using your holiday time and then you wouldn't be back.'

She showed him through to the living room and indicated for him to have a seat. He chose one of the bar stools. 'Can I get you a cool drink?' she asked.

'Just water, please. It's going to be another hot one,' he said, looking out of the window.

She poured him a glass and put it on the table, sitting opposite him.

'I was gutted about Angela,' he said. 'And Colin too. Now you're leaving, and I'm losing the best team I ever had. Such sad times. We could have gone on to better things.'

'You might have if you weren't drug dealers,' Myra said.

'Drug dealers? What are you talking about, Myra?'

Myra looked at him for a moment. 'William, Angela told me everything.'

'I really have no idea what you're talking about.'

There was silence between them, then another figure entered the room.

'I think you do, Mr Potter,' Bracken said. 'When Marcus King was being led away earlier this morning, he made a comment that made me think. He wasn't the mastermind behind all of this. Neither was Angela. She had made it clear that there was somebody orchestrating this whole thing. There could only be one person who was able to have the trial batches made up for the drugs you planned to sell.'

'You know, this is preposterous. I won't stay here and listen to this.'

Bracken took a step closer. 'Is it? We have teams searching your house right now. We're searching your lab. Yes, that search warrant was a little bit more difficult to acquire, but there are people from the American military on hand to oversee things, and they're just as appalled as us that you were using government money.'

William Potter laughed. 'This is a fairy story. You know Myra is involved in all of this. She set it up with her friends, Angela and Colin. We used to go out for a drink after work, but that was just as colleagues. I don't know anything about being a drug dealer.'

'Both Marcus King and Terry Jones are at the station being interviewed, each of them blaming the other. But guess what? What do they both have in common? You. They're both telling us about you.'

'You're going to listen to a couple of numbskulls

making up stories, trying to save their own skin? The judge will laugh that out of court. Nobody's going to put me in prison.'

'Even if that were true, do you think the American military are going to let you screw them out of millions of dollars? I mean, you had a tremendous budget, and yes, you delivered the goods, but Angela got greedy,' Bracken said. 'She didn't tell you that there's a flaw in the new drug. Even on the one you made for recreational purposes. She and Colin fudged the figures, and they told you it was working. But come on, William, you knew that already.'

'Did I?'

'Of course you did. You've been giving it to people without them knowing about it. Terry Jones, for one. And Professor Wall. He's the biggest mistake you made. He's like a caged tiger when normally he's very well spoken and has a lot of patience. So you knew there was something wrong, or thought you knew. Terry Jones said he would report back to you, and he did, but you told them you had to press ahead with the things as you'd already made the deal. But Angela knew it was far from fine. I'll bet Colin did too and they wanted more time, but there *was* no time. You had to get rid of them. How am I doing so far?'

'You're talking nonsense.' Potter stood up.

'One more thing: my team went with a search warrant to Marcus King's warehouse, where he stores his coffins. Guess what they found?' Bracken blocked the living room doorway.

'Wooden boxes,' Potter replied.

'Correct. And in one of them was a man called Dermot Shea. Or as Myra here likes to call him, *Beardy*. Myra was in a panic, thinking she had killed Dermot. Not true. He's very much alive and in a comfortable bed in the Royal Infirmary as we speak. Chatting away to my team.' Bracken looked at Myra. 'You didn't kill him after all, just knocked him out. But guess what? This idiot must have given him a Slo pill to see what effect it would have. He was out cold. Now he's very much awake and trying to cut a deal.'

'Bastard!' Potter said. 'I told him to kill those useless morons. The whole deal had gone through and we were ready to deliver this week. They were going to blow everything out of the water. So Shea killed them. He should have had Marcus deal with the corpses instead of leaving Colin at home. And putting Angela in the park! What was he thinking?'

They could see in his eyes that he had been taking his own medicine. His aggression was getting worse. He rushed at Myra, but Bracken stepped in his way and slammed a palm onto the man's chin, knocking him arse over elbow.

'Is Shea really alive?' Myra asked as Bracken rolled Potter over and handcuffed him. He turned and shouted and uniformed officers came in.

'I'm sorry, but Dermot Shea was found dead in one of the coffins. It's still self-defence, as your clock footage will prove.'

'What?' Potter said as he was dragged to his feet. 'You were lying? You bastard!' He struggled with the uniforms as they led him out.

'Your clock got the confession too. Nice work.'

THIRTY-THREE

A few days later

'Sunday roast. Nothing better,' Bob Long said.

'Here's to that!' Bracken said, and they all raised their glasses. The guests had all been taken care of and now it was their turn.

'Even Max likes roast beef,' Ed said. 'So I gave him a piece off your plate,' he said to his son.

'You'd better start liking tofu, old man, because you'll be getting that every night.'

'Oh, Sean, don't wind him up like that,' Mary said.

'He knows I'm only kidding.' Bracken smiled at his old man.

'So, let's raise a glass to Chaz's new job. First day tomorrow,' Bob said.

'To Chaz!' they all shouted, clinking glasses once again.

'Thank you all so much. I was on the fence about starting in the lab at the Royal, but being drugged pushed me over the edge and made the decision all that much easier.' She smiled at them all with a tear in her eye.

'Good for you, love,' Ed said.

'Yes, good choice, Chaz,' Kara said.

'And you've not had any side effects?' Natalie Hogan said, ever the doctor.

'I'm fine, thank you,' Chaz smiled, putting a hand on hers.

They all ate, shared some jokes and chatted in general, and then they mucked in to clear the debris of Sunday dinner away.

Then Bracken and Chaz went for a walk with Max.

'Are you going to miss working in the mortuary?' Bracken asked.

'A little bit.'

'Onwards and upwards, though, eh? More pay, and you're the boss.'

'And I don't have to work with Terry Jones. He

was always a pain in the arse anyway. And I only have to be on-call every so often.'

'I'm proud of you, Chaz.'

'I know you are.' She laughed and gripped his arm tighter. They walked down Station Road towards the High Street and St Margaret's Park.

'How's the flat hunting coming along?' she asked.

'Have you seen the prices of houses these days?' Bracken countered.

'Yes, I have.'

'It seems like every place that goes up for sale is demolished and flats or houses are built on it. And they're not cheap.'

'Unlike you, who is very cheap.'

'Listen, I just want a nice place in a nice area.'

'There *is* an alternative, you know.' They walked past the church and the graveyard at the bottom of the road.

'Oh yeah? What's that? Join a cult? Run away to the Navy?'

'You know fine well what I'm talking about. You could move in with me.'

He nodded but didn't make eye contact. 'That's one possibility.'

'Are you scared to make the move? Moving in

with the girlfriend who might make unjust demands of you?'

'First of all, I told you right off the bat I need a twenty-four-hour turnaround. And it's not that. Sometimes, things are ticking along nicely, then people change things and that messes up their relationship. I don't want that to happen to us.'

She stopped for a moment. 'Just promise me you'll think about it. It might not happen next week, but maybe one day.'

'I will.'

AFTERWORD

Now we've reached the end of Bracken #4 and I hope you enjoyed it.

The church on Holyrood Road may or may not still be there, but as far as I know, it isn't connected to the university. I used literary licence again.

Thank you goes to Charlie Wilson, my editor, for her hard work. She's a dream to work with. Thanks to Jim Brown for being a good sport in letting me use his name for a new character. Thank you to Jacqueline Beard. Your Eagle eyes are wonderful.

Thank you to my advance readers. If you would like to be a part of the team and get an advance copy of each new book – Harry McNeil and Sean Bracken – then message me on Facebook. All I ask in return is that you consider leaving a review on Amazon or Goodreads.

Thanks as usual go to Deb for looking after our fur babies while I work. And to my daughters, Stephanie and Samantha. Thanks also to Lou, Christine and Nick.

Last but not least, thanks to you, the reader. And while you're here, could I ask a favour? If you could spare a minute to leave a review or a rating for this book, it would be greatly appreciated. Thank you in advance.

All the best my friends.

John Carson

August 2021

New York